***"Are you going to lecture me again?"
Curt demanded.***

***"Are you going to listen this time?"
Jessie replied.***

"I always listen, Jessie." His voice turned husky. "But I pay attention to your actions more. Like when you kissed me."

"I think we should forget that kiss," she said firmly.

"I'm going to have to decline that request."

"It wasn't a request," she shot back. "It was an order."

"We're no longer in Daddy Boot Camp. So you're no longer in a position to be giving me orders."

"I'll come watch Blue dance," Jessie told him. "But don't go getting any other ideas."

Not get ideas? About Jessie? Impossible!

Dear Reader,

Silhouette's 20th anniversary celebration continues this month in Romance, with more not-to-be-missed novels that take you on the romantic journey from courtship to commitment.

First we revisit STORKVILLE, USA, where a jaded Native American rancher seems interested in *His Expectant Neighbor*. Don't miss this second book in the series by Susan Meier! Next, *New York Times* bestselling author Kasey Michaels returns to the lineup, launching her new miniseries, THE CHANDLERS REQUEST.... One bride, *two* grooms—who will end up *Marrying Maddy*? In *Daddy in Dress Blues* by Cathie Linz, a Marine embarks on his most terrifying mission— fatherhood!—with the help of a pretty preschool teacher.

Then Valerie Parv whisks us to a faraway kingdom as THE CARRAMER CROWN continues. *The Princess's Proposal* puts the lovely Adrienne and her American nemesis on a collision course with...love. The ever-delightful Terry Essig tells the tale of a bachelor, his orphaned brood and the woman who sparks *A Gleam in His Eye*. Shhh.... We can't give anything away, but you *must* learn *The Librarian's Secret Wish*. Carol Grace knows...and she's anxious to tell you!

Next month, look for another installment of STORKVILLE, USA, and THE CHANDLERS REQUEST...from *New York Times* bestselling author Kasey Michaels. Plus, Donna Clayton launches her newest miniseries, SINGLE DOCTOR DADS!

Happy Reading!

Mary-Theresa Hussey

Mary-Theresa Hussey
Senior Editor

Please address questions and book requests to:
Silhouette Reader Service
U.S.: 3010 Walden Ave., P.O. Box 1325, Buffalo, NY 14269
Canadian: P.O. Box 609, Fort Erie, Ont. L2A 5X3

Daddy in Dress Blues

CATHIE LINZ

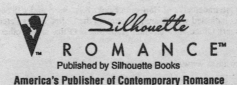

Silhouette

R O M A N C E™

Published by Silhouette Books

America's Publisher of Contemporary Romance

Acknowledgment: Special thanks to Sergeant Major Robin D. White, USMC, 2d Battalion, 24th Marines
for his assistance with all things U.S. Marine. Semper fi!
And per my marching orders, a very special thanks
also to Susan and Jimmie.
This book is dedicated to all the men and women who have so honorably protected their country by serving in the armed forces, including my father—U.S. Army, WWII—
and my brother, U.S. Navy, Vietnam war.

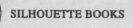

SILHOUETTE BOOKS

ISBN 0-373-19470-6

DADDY IN DRESS BLUES

Copyright © 2000 by Cathie Linz Baumgardner

Visit Silhouette at www.eHarlequin.com

Printed in U.S.A.

CATHIE LINZ

left her career in a university law library to become a *USA Today* bestselling author of contemporary romances. She is the recipient of the highly coveted Storyteller of the Year Award given by *Romantic Times Magazine* and was recently nominated for a Love and Laughter Career Achievement Award for the delightful humor in her books.

Cathie enjoys spending time with her family, her two cats, her trusty word processor and her hidden cache of Oreo cookies!

Dear Curt,

*Blue seems to have added me in the
family picture she drew in preschool today.
I think we have a problem....*

Jessica

Chapter One

Out of all the classrooms in all the preschools in Chicago, *he* had to walk into hers. Curt Blackwell. Even his name conjured up deep and dark memories.

The years hadn't been kind to him, Jessica Moore noted. But then kindness and Curt Blackwell had never had much in common.

Twelve years. It had been twelve years since she'd seen him. They dropped away in an instant.

Multiple images hit her as she stared at him with quiet dread. He was a study of contrasts. The rigidity of his cropped dark hair and crisp military attire were at war with the sensual fullness of his mouth and the heated intensity of his brown eyes. He'd always had the ability to consume her with a single glance.

She was surprised by how much he'd changed and yet still remained the same. He'd obviously stayed in the Marine Corps and the dress blue uniform looked good on him. Better than good.

There was a U.S. Marine Reserve Training Facility not far from here. She passed it on her way home every night, but she never dreamed that Curt would end up there. The last she'd heard, he'd been in some hot spot overseas.

Her eyes sought out the little things she remembered about him, like the scar near his right temple—the result of a dispute between him on his motorbike and a tree. The tree had won, he'd once told her. But he wore new scars now, including a fairly recent one that formed a ragged line along his jaw.

Despite the years that had passed, Jessica had recognized him immediately. But she saw no similar recognition on his part, which didn't surprise her. Curt had a track record of not seeing her. Only a few weeks after sharing the most incredible night of her life with her, he'd acted as if she were invisible.

Thrusting that humiliating memory out of her mind, she focused her attention on the little girl who stood nervously beside him, close enough to touch him but not doing so. Instead the little girl's hand was clutching the hand of the preschool's director, Sarah Connolly.

"We've got a new student here at the Happy Days Preschool and Day Care center," Sarah cheerfully announced. "This is Blue Blackwell, she's three years old, and she's just moved here from San Diego. And this is Curt, her father."

Curt's daughter? In her class? The magnitude of the pain caught Jessica by surprise.

Pull it together, idiot, she fiercely ordered herself. *You can't fall apart. Not here. Not now.*

Years of dealing with crises allowed Jessica to

make a fairly smooth recovery as she leaned down to the little girl. "Hello, Blue. We're glad you've joined us."

"Yeah, well, I'll leave her in your hands," Curt said uncomfortably, clearly eager to follow Sarah as she left.

Much as she wanted him to disappear, she had Blue's welfare to think of. The little girl would be terrified if Curt just dumped her off in a strange environment.

"You'll be joining us too, Mr. Blackwell," Jessica stated, using her best teacher voice, the one that said *I mean business.*

Apparently it had little affect on a Marine, because he just shrugged off her words and kept heading to the door. "I've got to get back to work," he was saying. Was there an edge of desperation in his voice or was she imagining things?

Jessica had no choice but to put her hand on his arm. By now she was so numb with shock that she didn't even register the physical contact. All she noticed was that it stopped him. "This will only take a few minutes, but it is necessary and extremely important for your daughter's comfort."

"Okay—" he shot an impatient look at his watch "—but I don't have much time."

Satisfied that he would stay, Jessica quickly dropped her hand from his arm and returned her attention to Blue. "My name is Jessica, and I'm going to be your teacher."

The little girl just nodded but didn't say a word. Blue's brown hair was tied up into two lopsided pigtails. Her blue jeans and white T-shirt were crisp with newly bought stiffness, and her black patent shoes shone. She wore a beat-up lime-green thin jacket better suited for San Diego than the chilliness of late March in the Midwest. She didn't appear to have a backpack or any school supplies yet.

After introducing Blue to the rest of the class as well as Jessica's two teaching assistants, Lisa Yu and Tawanna Houston, Jessica teamed Blue up with another little girl, Susan, who was the most outgoing in class and had the biggest heart. "Why don't you show Blue where she can put her coat?" Jessica suggested to Susan. "Then we'll begin story hour, and Blue can sit next to you."

Once the two girls had moved away, Jessica spoke to Curt in a quick undertone. "You can't just sneak out after leaving Blue in a new classroom. I want to make sure that she knows you're coming back for her. You need to tell her that. If you sneak out, you're breaking the trust she's placed in you." *Just like you broke the trust I placed in you all those years ago.* The thought streaked through Jessica's mind before she shoved it aside. She refused to give in to the past. She had a job to do here. "It would have been best if her mother could have been here with you," Jessica added.

"Her mother is dead," Curt said.

She blinked at the terseness of his announcement and the lack of emotion with which it was delivered. "I'm sorry to hear that, but in that case it's even more important that you don't sneak out on Blue. You're all she's got, and she needs to know that even though you're leaving now, you'll be coming back for her later."

He shifted impatiently. "Why can't you tell her that?"

"Because I'm not her parent, you are."

The noise level in the room suddenly rose as the small group of preschoolers sensed their teacher's distraction and decided to make the most of it. Grabbing the sheep off her desk, the one with a big brass bell around its furry neck, Jessica shook the sheep and made the bell ring.

Recognizing her quiet signal, all the students made the universal shush signal. Except for the class hellion, four-year-old Brian, who rushed forward to tug on Curt's sleeve. "Do you drive a tank? Are you stronger than Hercules?"

Curt just stared at the boy as if he were an alien creature before saying, "I left my tank at work. And I need to get back to it now," he added with a pointed look in Jessica's direction.

"Then we'll leave you alone so you can talk to Blue for a minute," Jessica replied with a looked just as pointed. "Come along, Brian. Which book do you think we should read for storytelling today?"

Although she stepped aside to give Curt and his daughter some privacy, her classroom wasn't big enough, nor Curt's voice soft enough to prevent her from hearing what he said to Blue. "Okay, here's the plan. I'll be leaving you at this facility and will return to pick you up at fifteen hundred hours."

It was as if Curt were speaking to one of his recruits, not a child. The man clearly didn't have a clue how to deal with his daughter, who just stared at him while nervously nibbling her lower lip.

Gathering her up into a hug as Curt made a hurried

departure, Jessica said, "You're going to be having lots of fun with us, and you'll be seeing your daddy again before you know it."

"He don't like me," Blue whispered unsteadily.

"Oh, honey, what makes you say that?"

"He said so."

Curt was behind schedule and he hated it. He prided himself on getting the mission accomplished— whether it was peacekeeping in Bosnia or registering his kid in preschool.

His *kid*. He still couldn't get over the fact that he had a daughter.

It had been a hell of a week. On Monday he'd gotten the final report from the medics informing him that the slight limp the Serbian sniper's bullet had left him with would most likely be permanent and would result in his being reassigned to a desk job. Frustration at his reassignment gnawed at him. He was a doer, not a damn paper-pusher.

And what had Fate done to help him out in his time of need? Delivered an almost-baby daughter he hadn't even known he'd had on his doorstep. That had only been three days ago.

The child welfare worker had filled in the blanks. It seems that Gloria, the earthy cocktail waitress he'd had a short interlude with in San Diego nearly four years ago before he'd been transferred and shipped overseas, had had his baby.

Curt was no idiot. He'd known that Gloria had a thing for Marines and that he hadn't been the only man in her life. But it had only taken one look at the little girl to know she was his. The strawberry-colored birthmark just above her knee matched the one he had on his own leg.

The kid was his. He had a daughter.

Presto, he was a father.

Curt knew he was totally unqualified for the job. He hadn't known his own father, who'd taken off before he was born. But Curt wouldn't take off on Blue. He wouldn't desert her. He lived up to his responsibilities. He was a Marine, by God.

Not that his uniform had impressed Blue's teacher. She'd looked at him as if he were pond scum. And ordered him around. Curt wasn't used to taking orders from a civilian. And he hated feeling like a raw recruit who was incompetent.

So he was no pro at this parenting stuff. How hard could it be? He was a member of the United States Marine Corps with a legacy of duty, strength, sacrifice, discipline and determination. He had a feeling he'd need all those things and more to measure up in that disapproving teacher's book.

The minute Jessica let herself into her Lincoln Square condo, she kicked off her shoes and grabbed her portable phone. She dumped her tote bag filled with school work on the floor before sitting on the denim couch. The blue corduroy jumper she wore was baggy enough that she had lots of room to curl her legs beneath her, a pose she resorted to whenever she was extremely nervous.

Normally she'd change into comfortable sweats as soon as she got home, but today she needed to talk to her best friend, Amy Weissman before doing anything else. She'd known Amy since they'd shared a freshman English class in high school.

"You'll never guess who walked into my classroom this morning," Jessica said. "Curt Blackwell."

"Curt 'Bad Boy' Blackwell?" Amy's voice reflected her disbelief. "From high school?"

"The one and only." And he'd been Jessica's one and only in more ways than one. The only one who'd captured her heart with the total surrender of first love. The only one she'd given her virginity to. The only one who'd ever kicked her in the teeth afterward.

She didn't have to vocalize any of those things to her best friend. Amy already knew. "Tell me he's come crawling back to you after all these years, and you shoved his tonsils down his throat," Amy growled, never one to be docile in her defense of her friends.

"Not exactly. He didn't even recognize me. He came to register his daughter in my preschool class."

"Oh, Jessica, I'm so sorry."

Jessica closed her eyes and saw herself as a senior in high school, the nerdy brain and social misfit, the only girl in her class who didn't have a date for the prom. And then there was Curt, the bad boy she'd had a crush on since her freshman year. When she'd run across a tipsy Curt behind the public library on prom night and he'd flashed his wicked smile at her, she'd finally given in to her feelings and they'd ended up making love in the back seat of his beat-up Mustang.

She could still remember the smell of fresh-cut grass drifting through the open window of his car, the scratchy feel of the cracked vinyl of the seat against her bare thigh, the sound of her name on his lips and the heat of his hand on her skin—the forbidden passion and the incredible outcome. Her only thoughts had been of him, her only wish to be with him.

But the next day Curt was gone. The United States Marine Corps had a prior claim on him.

Even though he'd left, Jessica had been sure that Curt would write to her from boot camp. He didn't. She didn't panic. Not until she skipped her period. *Then* she'd panicked.

Curt had come home for a few days after completing boot camp, but she'd only found out he was back thanks to a chance meeting on the street. When he didn't even speak to her...when he instead turned away from her with an embarrassed look on his face, her heart and her foolish dreams of a future with him had crumbled.

Her period had started the next morning, the pregnancy scare over. She'd eventually gotten over the feeling of betrayal. But when he'd walked back into her life, the past had come rushing right at her. If she really had been pregnant all those years ago, she and Curt would have had a child together. A daughter maybe. Would she have looked like Blue?

"What are you going to do?" Amy softly asked, bringing her back to the present.

Jessica took a deep breath before replying. "I'm going to teach his daughter. I'm a professional. I won't blame the child for the sins of the father. And that little girl really needs someone to help her. Curt is still in the Marines, and he treats her like she's a recruit instead of his daughter. And she's such a sweet little girl."

"What happened to her mom?" Amy asked.

"She's passed away, that's all I know. I can't turn my back on Blue," Jessica said firmly. "First and foremost she's a person in her own right. And she deserves to have someone care about her, especially after what she's been through. Curt only got to me today because I didn't see him coming. There's no way in the world that I'd ever let Curt Blackwell close enough to hurt me again."

"Do you need any help getting ready for bed?" Curt asked Blue. He'd already learned from experience that she was much better at undressing than dressing.

She shook her head.

"Okay, then I'll be in your room for lights off in five minutes."

He sighed as she scurried from the room. He'd tried talking softly to her, but it didn't seem to make any difference. He hated the possibility that she might be afraid of him, but had no idea how to rectify things.

Rubbing the back of his neck, he stared at the pile of paperwork that still needed completing by the morning. The government liked everything done in triplicate and that included forms. The five minutes he'd given Blue went by in the blink of an eye. When he walked into her room, she was waiting for him, sitting in her bed as erect as any seasoned Marine.

"At ease," he told her.

She blinked at him and relaxed a bit. She should be happy. He wished she'd be happy. Hell, the kid had a bedroom fit for a princess. He'd let her pick out everything herself, partially because he didn't have a clue what a three-year-old would like and partially to please her.

She was his daughter, but she was still a stranger to him. Maybe if he'd been in her life from the time she'd been a baby, maybe then he'd be a pro at this daddy stuff by now.

As it was, he was feeling totally out of his element here. The kid had such sad eyes. Brown like his. And she rarely smiled. She did grin when he did his Three Stooges impersonations, but he suspected that was just because she got a kick out of him making a fool of himself.

Like he had with that teacher today. For some reason she'd looked familiar to him, but he couldn't think why. He wasn't even sure of her name, at the time he'd been so rattled that he hadn't been paying much attention except when she'd ordered him to stay put.

Having briefly served as a drill sergeant, he'd recognized the steel in her voice. He could clear an entire room or dismiss a group of recruits with a single barked order. He'd been careful not to use that tone of voice around Blue. And not to swear. It wasn't easy sometimes.

As he looked around Blue's room, a host of Disney characters stared back at him from just about every surface—from the lamp shade to the sheets. He didn't know who the characters were, but Blue did. He'd been lucky that this two-bedroom unit had been available and in the same building as the furnished studio apartment he'd just rented on a monthly basis—before he'd known about Blue. The landlord had been willing to transfer the lease to this larger place.

"So you're all set for bed then, right?" he said.
Blue nodded solemnly.

"Do you need anything?" he asked.

"Fooba."

Curt reached for the grungy teddy bear propped against the foot of her bed. He'd offered to buy her a new bear but she'd insisted on keeping this mangy-looking thing. He suspected it was because her mother had given it to her.

He reached out, planning on smoothing Blue's ruffled hair...before he chickened out and reached for the switch on the Disney lamp instead.

"Good night then," he said.

"My shoes is shined," Blue suddenly announced.

"I...uh...that's nice."

She lifted the sheet to show him the black patent leather shoes she was still wearing.

Jeez, what kind of father was he to send his kid to bed with her shoes on?

"Now they's like yours," she said proudly.

"Yes, they are, but even I don't wear my shoes to bed. Let's take them off, you little monkey."

"I's not a monkey," she said solemnly. "I's a girl."

"You sure are."

"Would you like me more if I's a monkey?"

Imagining her trying to swing from the canopied bedposts, he hurriedly said, "No, I certainly would not like you better if you were a monkey."

"Oh." She sounded disappointed.

"I think staying a little girl is a wise move," he said, fumbling with the sissy strap on her shoes. He felt like a bull in a china shop. His hands were so big and her little girl stuff was so tiny. The first time he'd had to help her with her clothes it had taken him an hour to get her dressed.

Finally he got the shoes off her feet and tucked neatly beneath her bed. "Okay, now you're really ready for bed, right?"

Blue nodded.

"Good."

"But Fooba isn't," she added.

Curt sighed. It was going to be another long night.

The next afternoon, Curt was once again in Jessica's classroom, to pick up Blue after work. He was running five minutes behind schedule, but he should be able to make that up on the drive home providing he wasn't delayed...

"Mr. Blackwell, I'd like to speak to you in private for a moment."

The teacher. Glaring at him.

Curt sighed. There went his schedule.

Jessica heard him sigh, and the fact that he made her feel as if she was being a nuisance didn't endear him to her any. Too bad. If he'd filled out the parental information forms about Blue's likes and dislikes that Jessica had sent home with the little girl yesterday, then Jessica wouldn't have to speak to him today.

No, that wasn't entirely true. She'd still need to discuss with him what Blue had said about Curt not liking her and his having told her so. The little girl's offhand comment had sliced Jessica's heart. She wasn't eager to spend any time with Curt, but she couldn't turn her back on Blue. It was Jessica's responsibility as her teacher to do what she could. Even if that meant dealing with Curt.

Today his Marine uniform consisted of khaki green slacks and a khaki shirt. It made her wonder what he looked like in a black T-shirt and jeans. Don't go there, she warned herself. Keep your mind on Blue.

But before she could bring up the matter of the missing forms, Curt said, "What's the problem? Has Blue been misbehaving?"

"On the contrary," Jessica replied. "She's very careful not to do anything wrong."

Curt's relieved smile reflected his approval. "That's good."

"No, it's not. Not when it means that she's terrified of doing something wrong. She thinks you don't like her."

"I like the kid well enough," Curt replied defensively, "and I never told her any differently."

"So you never told her that you didn't like her?"

His "No, ma'am" was a Marine bark.

"Perhaps she overheard you telling someone else?" she suggested.

"No, ma'am." His narrow-eyed gaze told her he didn't appreciate this line of questioning.

"Have you told her that you love her?"

If she didn't know better, she could almost have sworn that Curt actually squirmed in his seat. "No."

"Why not? Children need to hear…"

"Look, I didn't even know she existed until a few days ago, her mother never bothered telling me. When she died, the authorities tracked me down and brought Blue to me. I've only known her a few days." Straightening his shoulders, Curt stared her right in the eye, his glance as steely as a double-edged sword. "Blue is my responsibility now, and I take my responsibilities seriously."

"I'm just trying to do what's right for Blue," Jessica assured him. "She needs attention and security."

"That's why I signed her up here. That's your job."

Jessica refused to give in to her anger. "She's looking for love and attention from a parent. From *you*. I realize that being a parent is a new situation for you. Our local community college has some classes that you might find helpful," she suggested.

"I don't need to go back to school," he stated in disgust. "I've handled much more responsibility than a little three-year-old kid." Seeing the expression on her face, he held up one hand and added, "I'm not saying I couldn't use a few pointers. But you can do that. You can teach me what I need to know."

Here it was. That fork in the road. Did she dare go down it with him? Even for Blue's sake?

What other choice did she have? "I'd be willing to work with you and suggest some additional reading," she said cautiously, "if you're willing to learn some additional parenting skills."

"Wait a second," Curt said, a lightbulb suddenly going on in those brown eyes of his as he leaned forward to stare at her as if seeing her—really seeing her—for the first time. "I know who you are."

Oh, no, not now. Not here. She wasn't ready for this yet.

"You're Jessie the Brain!" he said triumphantly. "We went to high school together."

Chapter Two

"Your hair was longer then, but you gave me the same speech about being 'willing to learn' when you offered to tutor me in Geometry."

Jessie the Brain. Curt couldn't believe that she was back in his life again after all this time. The last time he'd seen her was...

He frowned. It had to have been that night before he'd left to join the Marines. The memory was blurred by his having indulged in *way* too much alcohol that night. He recalled them bumping into each other and his surprise—first that he'd asked her to join him for a joy ride in his old red Mustang, second that she'd actually accepted, and third that he'd let her drive his car. They'd ended up in some park somewhere, and he'd kissed her...several times.

What happened after that wasn't clear. But the next morning, he'd woken with the worst hangover of his life. His temples throbbed just thinking about it.

As for the vague sense of guilt he was feeling, no doubt it was a result of the fact that he'd never gotten in touch with her again after that night.

At the time, he'd briefly wondered how far their making out had gone. Had he reached first base...or third? There was little to no chance he'd hit a home run and gone all the way—not with Jessie the Brain. She was a "good" girl, pure and demure. His total opposite.

Maybe this explained why she'd stared at him with such underlying hostility earlier. He'd probably made an idiot of himself that night, and she'd put him in his place when he'd tried to seduce her.

He looked at her with new eyes. Her honey-blond hair used to be longer, almost down to her waist. It was barely shoulder-length now, in one of those layered cuts that women these days seemed to favor. A hazy memory of him threading his fingers through her long silky hair flashed through his mind with the abruptness of an exploding land mine. He blinked at the unexpected vision. But when he tried to recapture the image, it was gone.

She had cat's eyes, tipped up at the outside corners. Leaning forward, he saw that they were an intense shade of green that reminded him of the jungles in the Philippines. Unless she was wearing colored contact lenses?

He cynically reminded himself that women had various ways of camouflaging themselves into something they weren't—everything from nose jobs to breast implants.

His gaze slid down her body with quick efficiency. She was wearing a pair of khaki slacks and a pink shirt. Nothing sexy there. Very practical attire. But beneath that no-nonsense outfit she had a Marilyn Monroe kind of figure that wasn't popular on TV and movies these days, but which any man preferred over skinny orphan looks. He'd seen too many skinny orphans during his tours of duty overseas. Their grateful looks and shy smiles when he'd handed out candy bars that he'd always kept in his pocket still haunted his sleep some nights.

Jessie the Brain wasn't the type of woman who'd haunt a man's dreams. There wasn't anything about her that really stood out, aside from those catlike green eyes. But there was something about her just the same, an inner strength combined with a warm heart.

Here was a woman who faced life head-on. Here was a woman not impressed by his uniform. Here was a woman staring at him with disapproval and dismay—the kind of look he'd gotten from a majority of the adults in his teenage life. Not looks he'd received lately.

"It's been a long time," he murmured.

She shrugged.

"Jessie the Brain." He shook his head, as if still unable to believe they'd run into each other again. "After all these years. Your hair is shorter now."

Her hand flew up to her hair as if guilty at being caught. "So's yours," she shot back.

He nodded with a sense of satisfaction. Oh, yeah, she was definitely the kind of woman who could hold her own.

"But getting back to your daughter." Her voice held a no-nonsense tone that made him smile for some reason. "I really do think it would be best if you took one of the parenting classes at the community college—"

He cut off her words with a sharp wave of his hand. "You already said you'd be willing to work with me. There's no backing out now."

"I wasn't trying to back out."

His look challenged her claim.

"Okay, maybe I was," she admitted. "Because I'm not at all sure of your commitment to learning and to working with me."

His narrowed gaze had made new recruits quiver in their boots. "You're questioning my commitment?"

She showed no signs of being intimidated. Instead she gave him a narrow-eyed gaze of her own. "Do you really think you can hack Daddy Boot Camp?"

"Just try me," he said.

"If I think for one minute you're slacking off—"

"I'm a Marine," he interrupted her. "We don't slack off."

"Fine." She grabbed a piece of paper and scribbled down a few things before handing it to him. "Read these books by the weekend. I'm busy on Saturday, but I have Sunday free. I'll put you through some parenting exercises then."

"Outstanding. Your place or mine?"

His place or hers? Which would be the lesser of two evils, Jessica wondered. Having him invade her domain, or venturing into enemy territory by going to his place? The practical side of her pointed out that if she went to his place, she'd have a chance to see for herself where Blue lived and under what conditions.

"Your place," she said crisply.

"Excellent." His voice was just as crisp. Frowning, he said, "Do you keep in touch with anyone from the old neighborhood?"

She didn't want to talk about the past, but his question was so innocuous that it would raise a red flag if she didn't reply. "Only Amy Weissman. I wasn't exactly the most popular girl in school." She was pleased to hear that her voice sounded matter-of-fact and displayed no bitterness.

Instead of commenting on her statement, Curt said, "So I guess you went on to college just like you planned? The University of Illinois was it?"

She was surprised he'd remembered that much. "That's right." She didn't want to talk about the past any longer. It was a part of her life she'd put into a sealed box and stored in a distant part of mind. That had worked until this man had walked back into her life. "But that was a very long time ago."

"Yeah," he agreed. "It was."

He gave her no indication that he remembered what they'd shared, that night of passion in the back seat of his car. He'd probably had so many women since then that he couldn't keep track of them all, she thought tartly. What had been a momentous occasion for her had clearly been nothing much to him.

That all too familiar stab of pain pierced her heart, as it had when he'd first walked into her classroom.

Get over it, she fiercely ordered herself. Keep your mind on the goal here, make things better for Blue.

The pain lessened, and she gazed at him without revealing her inner turmoil.

"I'll see you on Sunday then," she said in a dismissive voice.

"You certainly will, ma'am," he drawled, unfolding his lean body from the chair to give her a mocking salute before heading toward the door.

She couldn't help herself. She stuck her tongue out at him. It was juvenile and impolite, but it sure felt good.

Until he said, "I saw that." Not bothering to stop or turn around, he indicated the mirrorlike reflective surface of the window next to the door into her classroom. "Nice tongue," he added before exiting.

This time she waited until he left before throwing a crumpled ball of paper after him.

Just when she thought it was safe, he popped his head around the door frame to say, "Nice toss. For a girl."

"Nice compliment. For a Marine."

His smile indicated his appreciation for her quick comeback. "I think we'll get along just fine."

She'd thought so at one time. But not now, not again. Not in this lifetime.

Curt frowned at the pile of books strewn across the living-room couch. Who knew there was so much to learn about a three-year-old?

He shuddered with relief that he didn't have to deal with the chapters marked Potty Training. He was sure that would have brought even a tough guy like him to his knees. He could have managed if Blue had been a boy. Heck, the suggestions for boys had sounded like target practice, only this time the targets had been floating Cheerios in a toilet bowl instead of enemy forces in a battlefield.

But girls were different. Different in so many ways that it was all he could do not give in to the doubts prowling around the pit of his stomach, just waiting for him to screw up as he'd done so many times as a teenager. Being in the Marines had rid him of those feelings, or so he'd thought until Blue had shown up on his doorstep.

He refused to surrender to fear. Marines never surrendered. They survived. They overcame. They succeeded. Over all odds.

Or they regrouped to fight another day.

Jessie the Brain was coming here tomorrow. He tried to view the place through her eyes. It was clean. Scrupulously so. No easy feat with a kid who seemed determined to leave her toys all over the place, even stuffing things in his shoes and his briefcase.

At first he'd been pleased that she'd liked the set of small trucks he'd bought her. It wasn't as if trucks were a girly thing. Maybe he should have gotten her dolls or stuffed animals. But she'd liked the trucks and had played with them for hours. When she wasn't hiding them in his shoes or briefcase.

One thing was for sure, Jessie wouldn't be able to give him any demerits on the safety front. He'd had the entire place childproofed—from the kitchen and bathroom cabinets and drawers to the electrical outlets and the pull strings on the venetian blinds covering the windows.

Of course he had yet to master the art of bypassing the kidproofing to open some of the cabinets or drawers himself, but he'd learn. Just as he'd learned how to open childproof bottles of aspirin without taking a hacksaw to them.

Who knew an apartment could hold so much danger for a curious kid? And Blue was certainly curious. He couldn't even count the number of questions she asked him each day. How do tigers roar? Why are we people and not tigers? Why does your mouth go up when you smile? He just told her to ask her teacher.

Which led him back to Jessie again. It seemed a majority of his thoughts led him back to her. Looking down at the book on his lap, he tried to focus on the words. Play patterns. Good manners. Social graces. Yeah, right.

Turning the book over, he gazed at the title again. *The Complete Idiot's Guide to Parenting a Preschooler and Toddler, Too*. Was this Jessie's way of telling him he was a complete idiot? He supposed when it came to parenting, he was. But that didn't mean he had to like it. He was accustomed to giving orders, not taking them. Read these books. She'd issued the order like a drill sergeant.

As for this Daddy Boot Camp thing, he hoped she didn't expect him to hop to it like some raw recruit. Because he had no intention of playing that game. A man had his pride. And a Marine had ten times that much.

That was one of the reasons he loved being a Marine. His fellow officers understood him. His recruits obeyed him. Rules and regulations left no wiggle room for things like taming tantrums. And a part of him still didn't see why he couldn't apply the Marines way of doing this to this parenting deal. Discipline

and order were good things. Things that needed to be
learned early in life.

Maybe if his father had had a little discipline he
wouldn't have abandoned Curt when he was born.
There were times he wondered about the blood he'd
inherited from his unknown father. What kind of man
walked away from his responsibilities that way?

A man not worthy of the name.

Which didn't change the fact that Curt not only had
no parenting experience, but he had no family life
experience. Not that there was necessarily such a
thing as a normal family in today's world of divorce
and stepfamilies. But even those families had some
kind of experience of love.

Curt had no such experience. His mother had considered him to be a burden, she'd told him so often
enough before the state had stepped in and put him
in foster care when he was nine.

He'd never thought of being a parent himself. Absently rubbing his aching leg, he refused to be intimidated by the prospect of what might lay ahead. He'd
pick up some pointers from Jessie and move on.

All he had to do was think of this as a new form
of training. As a Marine he'd completed boot camp
when he'd first enlisted. Since then he'd completed
additional training in everything from surviving behind enemy lines to advanced infantry training
schooling.

He knew that fear of the unknown was the greatest
fear of all. So all he had to do was learn the tricks of
this parenting thing, and he'd be home free.

During the Sunday morning drive to Curt's apartment complex, Jessica almost turned around and

headed back home about a dozen times. She had to keep reminding herself that the faster Curt learned a few parenting skills, the sooner he'd become self-sufficient and not be requiring her assistance. Not to mention that it would make things easier for little Blue if she had a father who knew how to express his love for her.

Not that Jessica was an expert on affectionate dads. Heaven knew her own father had always been a complete enigma to her. An autocratic man, he did not know the meaning of the word compromise.

Sighing, Jessica stole a quick glance in her Ford Taurus's rearview mirror to check two things—first, if she'd nibbled off all her lipstick and second, if the left lane was clear for her to move into it. The lipstick was long gone and the traffic was solid.

Flicking her turn signal, she managed to slip in between a truck and minivan. Curt's directions had been precise down to the mile with everything listed with military precision—turn north on Foster Avenue, proceed for 5.6 miles then turn east at next intersection. There hadn't been any additional colorful play-by-play, like turning left at the doughnut shop on the corner. The directions were like the man himself. No-nonsense.

She wondered what had happened to the bad boy she'd known as a teenager? Had he changed that much?

Her curiosity wasn't personal. She was merely interested in human nature, that's all. The silent assurance made her feel less jittery as she pulled into the apartment complex's parking lot. The pale brick building was a new one and in good shape. All the windows had screens, important for preschooler safety.

Before getting out of her car, she touched up her lipstick, a restrained mauve that drew attention to her lips without making her look made-up. The periwinkle-blue pants and matching tunic-length top she wore was casual enough to make it appear that she hadn't dressed up for today, but fit her well enough to be a confidence booster. Her hair was gathered up and piled on top of her head, held in place with a silver hairclip given to her by a parent last year.

She'd brought a tote bag filled with materials to assist her with today's lessons. There was no assisting her racing heart as she knocked on Curt's door.

He yanked the door open and pulled her inside before she could say a word. She no longer had to wonder what he'd look like in a black T-shirt and jeans. That's what he was currently wearing, and the result was simply too darn sexy for comfort.

"What took you so long?" he demanded.

She frowned at him, her gaze having traveled up his muscular body to his face. "Is that a cherry you've got on your chin?"

Grabbing the kitchen towel he had slung over his shoulder, he hurriedly swiped his face. "I was giving her toast, and I let her spread a little of the jam around."

"She seems to have spread it more than a little," she replied, trying not to laugh at the picture of what appeared to be a rattled Curt.

He glared at her. "Aren't you supposed to teach her how to eat in school?"

"She eats just fine in school," she solemnly assured him.

"Then teach her how to eat just fine at home."

"Jessie, Jessie, Jessie!" Blue shrieked and came racing into the room, her hands smeared with cherry jam.

"Halt!" Curt barked. "Sit!"

"She's not a dog," Jessica said, her voice making it clear she disapproved of his tactics.

But they did work.

Blue stopped in her tracks and sank onto the floor.

"Hands out," Curt ordered.

Blue obediently stuck out her messy hands.

Using the towel he had slung over his shoulder, he tried to wipe her hands. Jessica could have told him that he'd need a damp cloth to get rid of all the stickiness, but she let him find that out for himself.

"I's not a dog. I's a girl," Blue declared.

"No kidding," Curt muttered.

The little girl tilted her head to look up at her father. "Would you like me more if I was a dog?"

Jessica's heart just about broke there and then. Kneeling on the floor beside Blue, she quickly assured her, "Oh, honey, we like you just the way you are."

Curt hunkered down beside them, still intent on cleaning up Blue's sticky hands and apparently blithely unaware of his daughter's emotional needs.

Jessica gave him a discreet poke in his side, right between the ribs. Her meaningful look finally spurred him into speaking.

"Yeah right. Just the way you are," he told Blue.

"Only cleaner. Now march back into that kitchen, young lady."

Blue almost poked his eye out as she saluted him, leaving a smear of jam on her forehead and then on his. But she showed no signs of heading for the kitchen.

"Help me out here," Curt growled in Jessica's direction.

"I'm just here to observe," she replied, wanting to tell him that Blue needed his unconditional love, not a love that was dependent on her being a spotlessly clean good girl. But it wouldn't be appropriate now, not with Blue present.

"To observe?" he repeated in disbelief. "How useless is that?"

"If you'd rather I went home..." Jessica turned as if to leave.

"Stay."

"I'm not a dog, either," she replied over her shoulder, one hand on the doorknob. "So don't try ordering me around as if I were one."

"*Please* stay."

He wasn't happy about having to ask politely, there was no mistaking that in the taut line of his jaw. But he did it.

She sighed. "Let's get to work."

"Let's play," Blue said.

"First you need cleaning up." Curt gingerly picked his daughter up, as if were a package he was hauling from one room to another. He didn't prop her against his shoulder or hold her in the crook of his arm. He simply lifted her—his hands spanning her waist, his arms outstretched—and marched her into the kitchen.

Jessica followed him. The living room only had a colonial-style couch in a beige-and-orange plaid that had either been a garage sale find or a sign that Curt was totally style-deprived. The only other piece of furniture was a large TV set. The man clearly traveled light. She wondered how long he'd been in Chicago? When he'd gotten the leg injury that caused him to limp? Why he'd made love to her and then acted like nothing had ever happened between them?

All off-limits subjects, she warned herself as she stepped into the kitchen.

Morning sunlight streamed through the large window over the sink. The cabinets were white as were all the appliances and the countertop, which had nothing but a coffeemaker on it.

Seeing her interest, he said, "I childproofed all the cabinets so she'd be secure in this residence."

"That's good." So Blue would be secure, but would she ever know what it felt like to have her father give her an affectionate bear hug? Or would she forever be taking orders barked out in a curt voice? Forever falling short of expectations set too high to ever be accomplished.

Jessica certainly knew how that felt. She didn't want the same thing happening to Blue. Didn't want to see the little girl's natural exuberance drained right out of existence. Blue had already had enough tragedy in her life, what with her mother dying. What she needed now was stability, understanding and lots of love.

Jessica's arms ached to hold the little girl, to give her the loving she needed. The only thing that held her back was the knowledge that she was already in way over her head. Besides the bottom line was that she was merely Blue's preschool teacher. Curt was the parent in this scenario.

Which only served to remind her of how she'd once daydreamed about what kind of father he'd be. During that pregnancy scare so long ago, she'd anticipated his reaction to hearing they'd made a baby together when they'd made love in the back seat of his Mustang. In her teenage fantasy he'd been surprised, and then he'd taken her in his arms and asked her to marry him. It wouldn't matter that he'd just joined the Marines. She'd wait for him.

How foolish she'd been. How dangerously naïve. She'd badly wanted a baby, wanted someone of her own to love. That hadn't changed. What had changed was Jessica.

She no longer had to worry about pregnancy scares. Not after being gently told a few years back by her elderly family practitioner that she had a badly tipped uterus, so badly tipped that it was extremely doubtful she'd be able to conceive.

So she'd closed the door on one dream and focused her attention on her work teaching preschoolers, never thinking that one day she'd be teaching Curt how to deal with his own daughter.

Chapter Three

Dismayed at the direction of her thoughts and at the unexpected sting of threatening tears, Jessica mentally changed gears. This wasn't about her or Curt, it was about Blue.

Tugging out the yellow legal pad of paper where she'd written up her notes, she consulted the first page. "Most Daddy Boot Camps are designed for new fathers with infants," she told him. "I've adapted a program to your special needs. I thought we'd cover the basics—eating, getting dressed, bathing and bedtime."

Startled, Blue looked out the window and practically howled, "*Noooo!* Not bedtime now."

"That's right, it's not bedtime now," Jessica agreed in a soothing voice. "Let me see your beautiful clean hands." Blue eagerly held them out for her appraisal. "Very nice."

"Very nice," Blue agreed with a nod.

"Looking good," Curt said, tossing the dirty towel into the sink.

"Looking good," Blue repeated.

"Is there any one of the areas I've listed that you're particularly having trouble with?" Jessica asked Curt.

All of them. But he wasn't about to admit that. Instead he said, "You might as well go over all of them. But I have a few questions for you first." Picking up a notebook of his own, he listed them in rapid-fire succession. "How often do you have fire drills? Are you trained in CPR and pediatric first aid? Is the school registered or licensed with the state?"

She appeared to be impressed by his questions. "I see you've been doing some reading as I suggested."

"That's right." He hated feeling incompetent, so he'd made it a point to find out as much as he could in the past few days. A lot of what he read he considered to be psychological babble. He was a bottom-line kind of guy. But he was encouraged to read that kids needed schedules and routines. So did Marines. The recruits he trained needed the discipline to follow orders.

Having a raw recruit overcome their fear of heights enough to finally rappel down a tower gave him a feeling of accomplishment. Maybe this was Curt's chance to overcome a fear of his own—the fear of being a parent. Overcoming fear was another big deal for a Marine.

Yeah, he liked looking at the process that way.

"Did you hear anything I just said?" she asked him in exasperation.

"Yes. You said you were trained in CPR and pediatric first aid, that the preschool is licensed by the state and that you have the required number of fire drills.'' Learning to concentrate on more than one thing at one time was another advantage he possessed over an average dad. Another thing the Marines had taught him. ''Now tell me the secrets of dressing.''

''Secrets, huh? You make it sound as if there's only one way of accomplishing these goals. There isn't. Sometimes it's learning by trial and error. What I can do is give you some suggestions. First off, I'd mention that Blue here is a little girl, not a sack of potatoes.''

''Blue is a little girl,'' Blue repeated proudly. ''Is not potatoes. Is not a dog.''

''Your point being?'' Curt demanded of Jessie.

''Just that you seemed a bit uncomfortable carrying her.''

That's because he was a man more accustomed to carrying an M-16 rifle than a kid.

''Show me. Please,'' he added.

''Just act naturally.''

''Easy for you to say,'' he muttered.

''Here...'' Jessica bent down to lift Blue in her arms, propping the little girl on one hip. ''Like this.''

''That's a girly way to hold a kid,'' Curt scoffed.

She raised an eyebrow at his tone of voice. ''Oh, so now you're the expert?''

''Here.'' He took Blue from her and after an awkward moment or two, shifted his daughter so that she was perched atop his shoulders.

''*Giddeeup horsey!*'' Blue shrieked, digging her heels into his chest.

''Be careful she doesn't use your hair as the horsie's reins,'' Jessica warned him.

"It's not long enough," he replied, clearly not concerned.

He was right. But since his hair wasn't long enough for her to take handfuls of, Blue instead grabbed hold of his ears.

"No grabbing of ears," he ordered, wincing slightly. "Do you read me, young lady?"

"Yessir." She tried to salute and in doing so almost fell off his shoulders. Lowering her, he gingerly propped her against one shoulder and held her in the crook of his left arm.

"Gotta go potty!" Blue loudly announced, whereupon he hastily lowered her to the floor as if she were radioactive.

"Need any help?" Jessica inquired, trying not to laugh.

"Who are you asking, Blue or me?" Curt said.

"Both of you."

"Blue can go to the bathroom on her own, thank God. The cabinets in there are kidproofed, too."

Jessica was pleased to note that he still kept a watchful eye toward the open bathroom door down the hallway.

During Blue's absence, Jessica thought this might be a good time to address the issue of emotions. "Blue needs to know that you'll love her no matter what, not just when she's all cleaned up or when she's a good girl. Remember that your child will look to you as a model of how to express emotions, so you need to make a point of expressing them honestly."

Emotions weren't something a Marine needed. In fact, in his mind they did nothing but get in the way. As for honesty, he didn't think Jessie really wanted him expressing his inner panic. No, giving in to fear never accomplished anything in his view.

"Blue needs to see signs of your love and affection," Jessica continued. "Various ways of doing that are giving her hugs and kisses to congratulate her when she completes a difficult task, or to console her when she cries, or to comfort her when something hurts."

"Is that what your father did for you?"

His question caught her by surprise. "No," she quietly replied. "Quite the opposite."

"Yet you seem to have turned out okay," Curt pointed out.

"Appearances are deceiving."

"So basically you're telling me that if I don't hug her at just the right time she'll be screwed up for life? Gee, no pressure there."

"I thought Marines were used to dealing with pressure," Jessica countered.

"Yeah, well, I still don't think parenting should be so complicated," Curt grumbled.

"Stick around, soldier. You ain't seen nothin' yet," Jessica drawled with a grin.

Sucker punched. That's how Curt felt. From nothing more than Jessie's unexpectedly saucy smile. Ambushed by a woman with eyes so green they put sunlit leaves to shame.

Jeez, he was getting downright poetic here. A bad sign.

Or was it? Since when had being with an attractive woman been a crime? Since he'd become a dad probably.

But this was the best of both worlds. In Jessie he

had a woman he was finding increasingly attractive, and a woman who knew how to take care of his daughter.

"I's done," Blue proudly announced from the bathroom. "I's flushing now."

"I've tried correcting Blue's grammar," Curt told Jessie, not wanting Jessie the Brain to think his kid was stupid.

"You don't need to worry or to correct her each time. Instead you could just repeat the words yourself, perhaps say I am done cleaning the kitchen, so she'll hear for herself how the words go together. It's a natural progression as two- and three-year-olds start stringing words together, often mimicking what you say."

"One of the reasons I now watch what I say around her," Curt admitted.

"Good idea," she replied.

Was the sunlight coming in through the window playing tricks or had that been a flash of attraction he'd just seen in her eyes? Curt wondered. Maybe Jessie had decided to stop holding a grudge against whatever it was he'd done back in high school.

Or maybe he was just imagining things.

He'd been on his own for so long that the thought of flirting with a pretty woman was enough to make his blood flow a little faster. This could get interesting, he decided with a sense of anticipation.

While Blue sat on the living room floor and played with her toys—an eclectic collection of trucks, dolls, and a well-worn teddy bear—Jessica put Curt through his paces.

"First things first," she briskly told Curt. "Let's

begin with emergency first aid. How much do you know?''

''Enough to give you mouth-to-mouth resuscitation,'' he drawled.

This sudden flash of the bad boy she'd known in high school caught Jessica by surprise. She'd let her guard down a bit and he'd snuck up on her with that comment.

Studying him provided suspiciously few clues as to what he was thinking. The teenage girl she'd been would have become flustered by his intense perusal of her mouth, but the woman she'd become ignored his provocative behavior.

Or tried to. She quizzed him on various possible scenarios that would require immediate medical attention. He had a pretty good basic knowledge, but needed specifics for pediatric care. And all the while her wayward heart kept beating a little faster. It certainly wasn't because she found the topic of a first-aid checklist exciting. No, it was because he'd given her a certain kind of look, the kind a man gave a woman he was interested in.

Things got worse when she handed him a refrigerator magnet with the toll-free number of the Poison Control Center on it. His fingers brushed hers and the resulting tingle of awareness traveled up her arm. A simple touch, a familiar reaction—but one she hadn't experienced since her high school days.

Oh, there had been men in her life since then. And she'd felt attraction before. But not this spine-tingling current accompanied by a deep-felt recognition that this person's touch felt right and deliciously wicked at the same time.

Flustered, she glanced down to consult her master list. "Uh, the next item on the agenda is mealtime."

"Is there a reason we've gone from emergency first aid to food? Makes me think you've tasted my cooking," Curt noted wryly.

It was hard not to smile. "What are you feeding Blue?"

"Candy and potato chips," he replied mockingly.

At her startled look, he added, "What? That's what you're expecting, isn't it? For me to fail."

"That's not true."

"No? Then why are you treating me as if I were some raw recruit who didn't know my...foot from a hole in the wall?"

"I'm sorry if you don't approve of my teaching style," she said stiffly. "I'm no expert at educating adults."

"And I'm no expert at taking orders from a civilian, but you don't see me complaining."

"That's because you're the one who needs my help."

"And you're the one who offered that help," he reminded her.

Offered? Pressed into duty was a more accurate description but she wasn't about to quibble over semantics. "I'm trying to help you, but it would be easier if you weren't so stubborn and didn't have such an attitude."

"I'm not the one with the attitude, you are."

"I am not," she vehemently denied.

"Are so," he taunted her.

"Am not!"

"Am not, am so, am not, am so, am not, am so," Blue said in a singsong voice.

Startled at hearing herself mimicked, Jessica had to laugh. "We did sound like a couple of three-year-olds," she noted ruefully.

"I am three," Blue proudly stated, holding up three fingers. "This old."

Jessica smiled down at her. The little girl was such a sweetie. "You certainly are."

"What did you do to G.I. Joe?" Curt's voice reflected his dismay.

"I made him pretty." Blue held the action figure up to show off the large flowered hat she'd put on it.

"G.I. Joe doesn't wear flowers," Curt stated with emphatic outrage. "All the other G.I. Joes would laugh at him. Put his helmet back on."

Blue looked at her father uncertainly before her big brown eyes slowly filled with tears.

"Jeeez." Curt exhaled as if someone had just stomped on his foot, or maybe even his heart. "No crying. Big girls don't cry."

"Sure they do," Jessica inserted. "It's okay to feel sad, honey." She scooped the little girl in her arms. "I think that G.I. Joe looks great in that hat."

Blue sniffed and hid her face in Jessica's neck. Which allowed Jessica to give Curt a look that would have scorched steel.

"Okay, big girls cry," he allowed. "Sometimes. But a Marine's daughter doesn't cry." He reached over to awkwardly pat Blue once on the back. "You're a Marine kid now and you can..." He'd been about to say chew nails, but then he reconsidered the wisdom of that, knowing how Blue tended to take everything he said literally. "And you're even more powerful than G.I. Joe. You're tougher than other kids."

Her tears stopped, and she held out her arms for Curt.

He took her, and his embrace was easier now than it had been when Jessica had first walked into the apartment. A second later Blue was giggling at Curt's Three Stooges impersonation. Or maybe he was making Jim Carrey-like funny faces. Whatever, it made Blue laugh.

"Come on, let's show Jessie how you can put away some of these toys." Lowering Blue, he pointed to the pile of toys his daughter had strewn around the living-room floor. "One, two, three, four," he said in softer version of a drill sergeant's voice. "Get those toys off Daddy's floor. Left, right, left, right. Move those trucks right out of sight."

Jessica waited until later that afternoon, when Blue had finally tired herself out and fallen asleep to approach Curt on the subject of toughness.

"I'm amazed how she's able to keep going as long as she does," Curt noted from the doorway to Blue's bedroom. His daughter was curled up on the bed, with her right arm around her teddy bear. G.I. Joe, minus the flowery hat, sat on her bedside table. "She was supposed to begin her nap at fourteen hundred hours. That was thirty minutes ago."

Returning to the living room with him, Jessica said, "Sometimes you have to be flexible. And you have to remember that she's barely three years old. She's a little girl, not a Marine. A little girl who's recently lost her mother."

"I'm aware of that," he said stiffly.

"Does Blue ever talk about her mother, about missing her?"

"She told me her mother is 'upstairs in heaven' and asked me if that made me sad."

"And what did you tell her? That Marines don't get sad?"

He glared at her. He hadn't put it exactly like that, but pretty close.

Jessica sighed, as if Curt's gaffe was to be expected. "That might explain why she's being so stoic about things. About not crying, about wanting to behave and not do anything wrong."

"That's a good thing."

"As I told you when we had that discussion at the preschool, Blue is terrified of doing something wrong. Maybe she thinks that if she misbehaves, you'll disappear or die the way her mother did. Or that you'll send her away. I'm not sure, but I think it's important that we do find out what she's thinking, what she's feeling."

"I'm no good at that kind of touchy-feely...stuff."

"Tough noogies," she retorted. "You'll just have to learn how to get good at it. Meanwhile I need some facts to work with here. Do you know how Blue's mother died?"

"I was told it was a car accident. She fell asleep at the wheel while driving home after work. She worked nights as a cocktail waitress at a club in San Diego. The social worker told me that Gloria had a number of her friends watching Blue and that she was accustomed to being apart from her mother."

"Even so, I'm surprised Blue hasn't mentioned her more. Have you brought up the subject?"

He looked at her as if she were nuts. "Why should I? Like I said, she knows Gloria is dead."

"Telling Blue that big girls don't cry will actually make it harder for her to mourn and get past her mother's death. You need to allow her to express her emotions."

"All right, already. I won't tell her that Marine's kids don't cry. I'll let the kid cry buckets if she wants to."

"And you'll hold her and comfort her if she should want that. And you'll reassure her that you're here for her long-term, no matter what. That she can count on you."

Not that Jessica had been able to count on Curt. He'd never bothered contacting her after that fateful night, hadn't been fazed by what had gone on between them. She'd been the one who'd been terrified she'd gotten pregnant. She'd been the one who'd waited for him to come back from boot camp, because informing him she might be pregnant wasn't something she felt right telling him about in a letter.

Why did he still have such a powerful impact on her, after all this time? She hadn't expected the chemistry to still exist. Not that Curt had pushed it. If he had, she'd have been out the door so fast his head would have spun.

Instead it had been a million small things—the intensity of his gaze as he'd listened to her, the lean strength of his fingers as he'd fumbled with his daughter's Mickey Mouse sipping cup, the sense of power he projected. The latter was something new, something he'd lacked in high school, and she suspected it came from his years as a Marine, accustomed to taking care of himself no matter what the situation. Here was a man who could protect in the most physical and fundamental sense of the word.

Couple that with the occasional flare of his bad boy tempting sex appeal and it made for a very potent package.

He'd been her first love, and she supposed that those poets who said you never forgot your first love were right after all. Even if that first love forgot you.

"Blue needs to know she can count on you," Jessica repeated. Some of the anger she was feeling, at her own vulnerability to Curt, came through in her voice.

"Are you mad at me about Blue or is it something else?" Curt demanded. "Because I've had the feeling since I first met you that you've been ticked off with me. Why is that?"

"You *first* met me back in high school," she reminded him.

"Is that why you're angry? Just because I didn't recognize you right away?"

Right away? It had taken him an entire *week!* "I never expected you to remember me," she replied honestly. At least, she hadn't expected it once she'd seen his blank look when he'd walked into her classroom. She'd expected plenty when he'd come back from boot camp. She'd expected him to smile at her, talk to her, kiss her, tell her that what they'd shared meant something to him, that he hadn't been feeding her a line when he'd told her how beautiful she was and how special. She hadn't expected him to completely ignore her, to turn his back on her.

Curt frowned. "If you didn't expect me to remember you, then what is the problem?"

He was the problem. Having him back in her life stirred up the old cauldron of emotions that she'd kept a tight lid on since then. But she couldn't tell him that. So instead she said, "The problem is that you're a father now and I'm not sure you realize what that means."

Her words stung him where he was the most vulnerable. "Are you saying that I'm not taking my responsibilities as a father seriously?"

"No, I'm not saying that at all. I'm just saying that I'm not sure you realize what a tremendous responsibility this is."

"Being responsible for the lives of forty-five Marines in my unit when we're under attack from enemy fire is a tremendous responsibility. Fatherhood is a piece of cake compared to that," he scoffed, a part of him hoping that if he said that often enough he'd come to believe it.

She gave him a look that was almost pitying. "You really don't have a clue, do you."

It wasn't a question so he didn't bother answering it. "I know what I'm doing," he stated. "And what small things I don't know, I can learn."

But could he learn how to love? That was the major question here. Because if he couldn't love Blue it didn't matter how much he knew about emergency first aid, he wouldn't be able to cure the ache in her heart caused by a father unable to love her as she deserved to be loved.

Jessica should know. She'd experienced it herself.

Jessica's father, a corporate executive, moved every year. Her mother never complained, saying that what was good for Jessica's father was good for the family. As an only child, Jessica found the moves very difficult. As soon as she made friends, she had to pack up and leave them.

By the fourth grade, she stopped making friends. What was the point? It would only end up with her waving at them in tears as her family's car pulled out of that particular driveway for the last time.

It wasn't until her father died of a heart attack, on the job, that the moves stopped. So did their income, as her mother discovered to her dismay that her husband was deeply in debt after having played the stock market in a highly speculative financial deal that had gone wrong.

Jessica had been thirteen, and just about to start high school. They'd had to move again, from the affluent western suburb of Naperville into the city where her mother had gotten a job. But Jessica had been able to stay at the same northwest-side high school all four years.

She hadn't been able to say so many things to her father, to ask him why he'd never been able to hug her or show her any affection. To ask him if he'd ever really loved her at all. To tell him that she'd loved him and was sorry she'd disappointed him.

"You don't believe me?"

Curt's aggressive tone of voice interrupted her thoughts. "Wha...at?" She blinked at him, retreating from the tunnel of memories.

"I said what small things I don't know about fatherhood I can learn and then you give me the silent treatment.''

"It wasn't you. I was thinking of someone else."

Her comment irritated him. For some reason he'd never considered the possibility that she'd have a life of her own now, with a man of her own. He'd checked her ring finger early on, before he even recognized her as Jessie the Brain. But the fact that she wasn't married or engaged didn't mean she wasn't going with someone.

"What's his name?" Curt demanded.

She blinked at him. "Whose name?"

"The guy you were thinking about."

"I don't care to discuss it. Now, getting back to Blue..."

"You're evading my question."

"No kidding," she retorted.

"What are you trying to hide? Unless you're going to try to tell me that you weren't thinking about a man?"

"I'm telling you that it's none of your business," she repeated, getting angrier by the second. "Where do you get off asking me personal questions anyway?"

"You asked *me* personal questions. Why is your life suddenly off-limits? Why are you so touchy?"

"I am not touchy. And if you must know, I was thinking about my father."

"Oh." His laugh was rueful. "I should have figured that out instead of thinking you were mooning over some guy."

Mooning over some guy? As in mooning over Curt? Did he think she didn't have a life of her own just because she didn't want to talk to him about it? "For your information, I *am* seeing someone."

"Seeing someone?"

His mocking tone of voice aggravated the heck out of her. "Why do you say it like that?"

"Like what?" he countered, moving closer to her as if daring her to step away from him and admit that he got to her.

"As if it weren't true." Refusing to give an inch, she tipped back her head to glare at him. She was so close she could see her own reflection in his brown eyes. "You don't believe that I'm seeing someone?"

"I don't believe how much I want to kiss you," he whispered right before his lips covered hers.

Chapter Four

She should have been prepared. She wasn't.

She should have pushed him away. She didn't.

She shouldn't have responded. But she did.

For a Marine, he moved with subtle sensuality. He didn't come marching in to lay claim to her mouth. Instead he stole in beneath the cover of her defenses, coaxing her into surrender with an erotic declaration of intent. His lips rhythmically brushed back and forth against her trembling mouth.

Tilting his head in the opposite direction, he targeted her mouth once more.

And then it was too late. Too late to be logical. Impossible to be coherent when excitement was surging through her body so rapidly that her entire being was flushed with it. Then he caught her bottom lip between his teeth, drawing it into his mouth to suck and nibble until she was moaning with pleasure.

The moment she parted her lips, he took advantage

of his victory to lay siege, his tongue darting out to taste her, to test her, to tempt her. The feathery caress against the roof of her mouth made her weak in the knees.

Is this pleasure worth the risk? Is he worth the pain he's caused you in the past? Do you really want to repeat your mistakes? Think of the pain he could cause you in the future. Do you want to give him that kind of power?

Finally her self-protective security system kicked in, giving her the strength to pull away from him.

"No," she answered her own unspoken questions. "No!"

"All right." He held out one hand to shush her. "I heard you the first time. You'll wake Blue."

Jessica felt as if she were the one who'd woken from an enchanted slumber, as if she were emerging from some kind of spell. She blinked rapidly to clear her vision and clenched her hands at the anger flaring within.

"How dare you think you can just grab hold of me and kiss me."

"I didn't grab you," he said. "I just kissed you."

Just kissed her. His words seemed to dismiss what had just occurred as an everyday happening. Well, it might be in his world, but it certainly wasn't in hers.

"Listen, I didn't come over here to be your little playmate." She shoved her notepad into her tote bag, so upset her hands were shaking. "I came here because I thought you were serious about wanting to become a better parent. Obviously I was mistaken." Slinging her bag over her shoulder, she made a beeline for the front door.

"Wait a second…"

"Daddy!" Blue's voice drifted out from her bedroom.

"Go take care of your daughter. If you're half as honorable as you claim to be, that's what you should be doing right now. And that's all you should be doing," Jessica told him before walking out.

"He did what?" Amy shrieked.

Jessica looked around the family-owned restaurant to make sure no one had overheard them but the sound of the Backstreet Boys on the radio had apparently drowned out Amy's exclamation. Dino's was located only two blocks from her condo and had been a neighborhood fixture since the seventies. Jessica had been coming here since she was in high school. On those nights when her mom had worked late, Jessica had come here to eat dinner because no one was a stranger at Dino's.

The decor was certainly not the main attraction. Everything was in varying shades of brown. Bottles of ketchup and mustard along with pink packets of sugar substitute supplied a little color on the fake wood Formica tabletops.

No, it wasn't the decor that kept the customers coming in. It wasn't even the lemon meringue pie, although that was superb. No, it was the ambience, the feeling that this place was a twenty-four-hour living room for the entire neighborhood. This was where you came just to talk. Or to celebrate, with a little comfort food, the small milestones that comprised your life. For Jessica, this was the place you came to order a cheeseburger and curly fries and dish the dirt with your best friend.

Lowering her voice, Amy leaned forward across the table in their booth. "You're telling me the man actually had the nerve to kiss you? So the sob story about him needing your help to be a better father was just a pitch to get you in his bachelor pad and have his way with you?"

Jessica munched on a curly fry. "Well, there's no denying the man needs help in the parenting department."

Amy shook her head and added salt to her burger. "That poor little girl."

"I'm not saying that he's arrogant and overbearing, even though he is. And I'm not saying that he hasn't come to care for his daughter and that he isn't trying."

"Yeah, he's trying, really *trying*. As in impossible."

Jessica shrugged. "I'm not even sure that he planned to kiss me. I mean, I don't think he'd go to all that trouble, reading all the books I told him to read, just to steal a kiss. What I'm saying, though, is that he took advantage of the situation."

"No kidding. I warned you about him."

Jessica nodded. "I know you did."

"And you told me not to worry, that there was no way you were going to let him get close enough to you to cause any trouble," Amy reminded her.

"Yes, well, that was the plan."

"He's using his daughter to get to you."

"That may be, but it doesn't change the fact that Blue really does need me."

Amy took another bite of her burger and swallowed it before speaking. "You said Curt read the books you gave him, right?"

"Yes."

"And you spent several hours at his place working with him on various parenting skills, right?"

"Right."

"Then I say the man's on his own. You did what you could to help Blue. But you can't put yourself at risk."

"It's ridiculous that I allowed myself to be so vulnerable," Jessica said in a voice filled with self-disgust. "But then who knew that after all these years I'd still be..."

"Still be what?"

"A pushover," Jessica replied morosely.

"Hey, don't be so hard on yourself." Amy patted Jessica's arm. "He's the one at fault here."

"I just wasn't expecting him to kiss me, and even if he did I wasn't expecting to...well...to enjoy it so much."

"Bad sign," Amy noted.

"Tell me about it."

"I think you need to spend some time with the new guy in your life. How are things going with Trevor?"

Trevor Locke was a financial advisor whom Jessica had been seeing for about a month. Recently divorced, Trevor wasn't ready to get into another serious relationship, which suited Jessica just fine. She preferred going slowly these days. "Things are going okay."

"Good. Glad to hear it. Maybe Trevor will protect you from Curt."

The image of Trevor, a nice enough man but no Arnold Schwarzenegger, going up against Curt, the ultimate lean-mean-fighting-machine Marine was enough to make her shake her head. "No, if I want protecting from Curt, I'll have to do it myself."

"What do you mean *if*. Are you considering getting involved with Curt again?"

"No. I told him I was seeing someone else."

"Before or after he kissed you?"

Jessica had to think a minute. "Before, actually."

"Ah."

She paused in the middle of reaching for another fry. "Ah, what?"

Amy shrugged. "The guy was jealous that you've moved on with your life."

"Moved on? I should hope so after twelve years. I haven't seen Curt since that summer when we were eighteen."

"Yeah, but in those twelve years you've never really gotten serious about anyone else."

"That is not true," Jessica protested. "There was Mike."

"Yeah, right. Mike, poster boy for the Peter Pan syndrome. Come on, he was never a real candidate for settling down."

"Okay, then what about Jeff?"

"What about him?" Amy countered.

"He was ready to settle down. I came close to accepting his proposal of marriage last year."

"Coming close only counts in horseshoes and hand grenades. Which brings us right back to Curt, poster boy for hand grenades and land mines in the personal relationship department. You know what?" In her excitement, Amy waved a curly fry at her. "I think the reason you didn't accept Jeff's proposal is that you've never really gotten over Curt."

Jessica almost choked on a bite of cheeseburger she'd just taken. "That's ridiculous," she declared, wiping mustard from her chin.

"Is it? Can you honestly tell me that you haven't wished that his daughter was yours as well?"

Jessica had to look away. Amy knew her too well.

Amy's expression was immediately filled with regret. "I'm sorry. I didn't mean to bring up painful memories…"

"Most of my memories of Curt are painful ones."

"Never a healthy sign in a relationship."

"We didn't really have a *relationship*. I tutored him in Geometry. He tutored me in having sex in the back seat of his car."

"If sex was all it was, you would have gotten over him by now."

"Okay, I admit that Curt was my first love and yes, there's something powerful about the first love in your life. But that kiss today was just a momentary lapse," Jessica firmly stated. "From now on, I'm determined to be immune to Curt's charm."

Amy grinned at her. "I never thought of Curt and charming in the same sentence. Not unless he's totally changed from the way he was in high school. Dangerous, tempting, provocative, powerful—those are descriptions I could easily buy. But charming? Nope, I don't think so. Sounds too smooth for Curt Bad Boy Blackwell. Unless he's gotten polished in his old age?"

"Hardly. He's as powerful as ever."

"Ah." Amy nodded her head knowingly.

"Not *ah* again. You never say *ahhh* like that unless you mean something, and it's usually something I'm not going to like."

"I think you're going to need a stronger vaccine against Curt than a pep talk with me over cheeseburgers and curly fries. I think you're going to need another man. The sooner, the better. Here…" Amy hauled her cell phone out of her purse. "Time to call in reinforcements. Call Trevor."

Curt tried to call Jessie several times Sunday evening but she didn't answer, and he didn't feel like leaving a message on her machine. What could he say? That he was sorry he kissed her? He wasn't.

He was sorry she'd lit out of here so fast. And he was sorry that Blue was upset at not having said goodbye. His assurances that she'd see Jessie at preschool the next day seemed to fall on deaf ears. His daughter required extra work getting her to sleep. He read her a Winnie the Pooh book and *Goodnight Moon* three times. In the end he'd been forced to read from his U.S. Marine Corps procedure manual, using the kind of monotone voice that had always made him doze off when his high school teachers had used it.

The thought of high school brought his thoughts right back to Jessie again. He wasn't sure why he'd kissed her. It had been an impulse. He certainly hadn't invited her over with that thought in mind. Or at least, he hadn't invited her with just that thought in mind. He had honestly wanted help with his daughter. And the trouble he had getting Blue to bed only proved to him that he still had a lot of ground to cover.

The same could be said of Jessie. Her response to his kiss had been more than he could have imagined, and he had a pretty good imagination. But then she'd gone all cold and backed away from him. Sometimes women weren't any easier to figure out than three-year-olds.

Catching sight of a copy of *The Complete Idiot's Guide to Parenting a Preschooler and Toddler, Too* still open on his couch, he couldn't help wondering if they had a had a version for dealing with women.

Not that he'd had many problems in the past. But then the type of woman he'd chosen hadn't made many demands. They'd only been interested in the same kind of no-strings short-term relationship that was his specialty. Jessie was different.

He'd known that even back in high school. Jessie the Brain had been as much an outcast as he'd been. Sure the reasons were different. She was the awkward class brain, and he was a foster kid with an attitude.

The whispered snubs had come early in his school years. Then came the shouted insults. Lots of derogatory words were used but they all basically meant the same thing—that he was illegitimate, poor, white trash who would never amount to anything. Bad seed, bad blood, the other kids' parents had muttered, shaking their heads and slamming their doors in his face.

By the time he was in high school he'd decided that if they wanted bad, he'd show them bad. If they wanted trouble, he'd show them trouble. He'd stayed clear of drugs and gangs, but had gotten involved in a few shady dealings. When his classes were over he'd also worked legitimate jobs flipping burgers, stuffing tacos, even working on cars. He didn't stay in one place very long. His employers claimed he had a bad attitude.

They weren't the only ones making that claim. In the end, his teenage years had been spent living in a group foster home. He'd always been a loner, never feeling he'd belonged. Until he'd joined the Marines. Now he felt part of something bigger than himself.

Being a dad didn't make him feel like he belonged. Instead it brought back those old feelings of insecurity and not being good enough.

When Jessie had tutored him, she hadn't made him feel stupid. She'd been the first one who hadn't judged him, who hadn't been afraid of him, who'd refused to cut him any slack, who'd complimented him when he succeeded and made him feel so good that he wanted to please her all the time.

She still had that ability. He'd learned that much today. That and the fact that she could kiss like an angel. A Victoria's Secret angel, he decided with a grin.

He ended up falling asleep on the couch, the book on parenting still spread across his stomach. His morning routine was disrupted by him waking up in the living room instead of in bed at his customary oh-six hundred hours. Breakfast was rushed, but Blue thankfully didn't spend her usual time dallying over her cold cereal. He got her to preschool right on time.

"Are you coming back?" she asked him as she did every day.

"Affirmative. I'll pick you up at this facility at seventeen hundred. Understood?"

"Uh-huh." Blue nodded before turning away from

him and rushing into her classroom yelling Jessie's name.

Curt was tempted to stay a minute longer and get a peek at Jessie himself, but he had a busy schedule ahead of him. He spent Monday mornings at the Great Lakes Naval Training Facility north of Chicago. Although the Marine Corps was a separate branch of the Armed Forces, it fell under the jurisdiction of the Department of the Navy and the Corps had never been real happy about that.

After returning from Bosnia, he'd gotten his physical therapy at Great Lakes. Now he'd been temporarily assigned to act as an instructor to new Navy recruits a few days a week. It was all blackboard stuff, not physical. And it was frustrating.

Four hours later, he'd finished his class and was sitting at a borrowed desk in a crowded room, filling out yet more paperwork, when someone slapped him on the back. "I never thought I'd live to see the day when the great Blackwell would be teaching squids, the lowest form of sea life."

"Wilder!" Curt leaped to his feet, his bum leg forcing him to hang on to the edge of the desk for a moment to regain his balance. "What are you doing here?"

Curt and Joe Wilder had been in boot camp together and had remained friends ever since. Joe was his opposite—a guy who got along with everyone, who'd grown up in a tight-knit military family. With his dark hair and blue eyes, the guy could melt female hearts with no effort at all.

Joe was also an inveterate practical joker so when

he started snickering as Curt sat down, he braced himself for the worst.

"What did you do?" Curt demanded suspiciously, checking his office chair to make sure all the wheels weren't about to fall off or something.

"Me?" Joe repeated with a choir boy look of innocence that Curt didn't trust for one minute. "Why, I didn't do a thing."

"Then what's so funny?"

"You had a class with a bunch of squids this morning, didn't you?"

"Yeah, why?"

"You get any unusual feedback?" Joe inquired. "A few snickers maybe?"

"Why? What's wrong?" He automatically checked his fly.

"Nothing. If you like yellow happy faces and giant flowers on the soles of your shoes."

"What?" Curt grabbed his shoe and tried to turn it so he could see the bottom. He groaned. "Oh, no."

"Am I correct in assuming that you didn't place those there yourself?"

Curt growled, "Zip it, jarhead. It must have been Blue." Then he tried in vain to peel the stickers off. The set of yellow happy faces proved to be especially stubborn to get rid of.

"Blue?" Joe repeated, obviously running the name through his mental little black book. "Is she that exotic dancer—?"

"She's my daughter," Curt interrupted him.

"Your daughter?" Joe repeated in disbelief. "When did that happen?"

"In San Diego almost four years ago. Remember Gloria?"

"Who doesn't remember Gloria?" Joe noted fondly.

"Yeah, well she had my baby and never told me about it. Don't give me that look. I used protection but something must have gone wrong. First I heard about Blue was when Gloria died, and I was listed as the kid's father and guardian."

"Hey, that's too bad about Gloria. She had a big heart. Listen, I hate asking you this, buddy, but are you sure..."

"That Blue is mine?" Curt completed for him.

Joe nodded.

"Yeah, I'm sure. She's got the same birthmark I had."

"Why did Gloria name her kid Blue?" Joe asked.

"Gloria always did have a thing for my dress blues, so I figure that's the reason Blue got the name she did. Damn, I can't get these stupid stickers off!"

At the sound of Curt's string of salty curses, Joe fixed him with a disapproving look that would have done a priest proud. "I certainly hope you don't talk like that around your daughter. When do I get to meet the kid? I think I like her already," Joe decided with a grin. "Anyone who gets under your skin is okay by me."

"With friends like you, Wilder, who needs enemies?"

"Anyone tell you that you lack a certain human trait known as a sense of humor, Blackwell?"

"Yeah, you did. Right after you put Heat in my jockstrap."

"I have no knowledge of the aforementioned incident," Joe claimed.

"Losing your memory already, Wilder?"

"Now that you mention it, I do seem to recall my completing a certain 4.2-second forty-yard sprint afterward with you hot on my tail." Joe chuckled. "I never knew I could run that fast. But you got even with me in the end."

"Hey—" Curt held his hands out in a motion of disavowal. "I keep telling you that I had nothing to do with you pulling that assignment in the Mojave Desert. How could I? I'm just a lowly Infantry Platoon Sergeant."

"Yeah, right. But at least sidestepping snakes in the desert isn't as bad as teaching squids."

Like most Marines, Joe felt a friendly rivalry with the U.S. Navy.

Leaning back in his chair, Curt fixed his buddy with a friendly glare. "Marines teach Navy SEALS."

"Now that you mention it, I'm on my way to Quantico myself for some special training. I had a few hours layover at O'Hare before my flight so I thought I'd take a cab up here to check in and see how you were doing. I had no idea I'd find out you were a dad."

"I'm not sure about this dad stuff."

"What are you talking about? You're a Marine. How hard can being a dad be?"

"Yeah, that's what I thought."

"So who changed your mind?" Joe asked, as shrewd as ever. "And what's her name and phone number?"

Curt's glare became a little less friendly. "Her

name is Jessie and she's my daughter's preschool teacher. Put your black book away, I'm not giving you her phone number.''

"She in the book?"

"Forget about it."

"Oh, so that's how it is." Joe nodded knowingly. "You've put a claim on her yourself. *Ooh-rah!*" Joe's version of the Marine motivational cry was accompanied by a comrade-at-arms thump on Curt's back.

"Change of subject now—"

"Only if it's something that will embarrass you as much as this subject does," Joe inserted with a grin.

"What happened to Semper Fidelis?" Curt demanded, reminding his buddy of the Marine motto, Latin for Always Faithful.

"Semper Fi." Joe used the shortened version. "Best motto of any branch of the Armed Forces."

Curt had to smile at his friend's brashness at singing the Corps praises in the midst of a Naval base. The looks they were getting from their Navy counterparts promised retribution. "Best uniform, too," he added. "Dress blues."

"Best haircut." Joe ran his hand over his head and his shortly cropped hair. "You can't have a bad hair day with a high and tight."

Getting in the swing of things now, Curt said, "Best slogan—Once A Marine, Always A Marine."

"Tell that to the Marines," Joe countered with a hoot.

"Send in the Marines!" they both shouted before being completely surrounded by their naval counterparts as the "friendly" pushing and shoving began.

Chapter Five

As Jessica sat across the table from Trevor at the Thai restaurant, she wondered why *he* couldn't be the one to make her heart beat faster. Instead she was having a hard time staying awake as he went into excruciating detail about his collection of Asian art.

It wasn't that she hated art. The problem was Trevor. And it irked her that she hadn't noticed it until Curt had reappeared.

A successful financial advisor, Trevor was a nice enough man, if a little overly impressed by his own intelligence and wealth.

They'd been dating for about a month now. At first Jessica had thought that as she got to know him better, the attraction would continue to grow. But it hadn't. There was just no real spark between them.

It wasn't as if she was looking for instant lust here, or for combustible chemistry. On the contrary, her experience with Curt had taught her that there was a reason passion was always described in terms of fire and flames—because it burned and destroyed.

No, she didn't want uncontrollable passion. But she did want something more than she had with Trevor. Surely it wasn't a good sign that right now she'd rather be sitting at home in front of her TV than sitting here with him. Or that the best thing about her evening so far was the spring rolls.

So much for Trevor protecting her from Curt's attraction. Amy had claimed it was time to call in reinforcements. The only thing tonight had reinforced was that she and Trevor didn't have much of a future.

Maybe you should have called in the Marines instead. Or one Marine in particular.

The thought bolted across her mental radar. It was the kind of thinking that had gotten her in trouble in the first place.

Maybe she should give Trevor another chance after all. But by the end of the evening, when he kissed her good-night, she knew there was no hope. Maybe he knew the same thing because he made no mention of going out with her again. After an awkward second or two, the sound of her ringing phone allowed Jessica to make a quick getaway into her condo.

Kicking off her high-heeled navy pumps, she curled her legs beneath her as she sank onto her couch and prepared to give Amy the sorry details of her date with Trevor.

But it wasn't Amy on the phone. It was Curt.

"You omitted a few important elements from that Daddy Boot Camp of yours," he said without bothering with more than a cursory greeting. "You never did get around to the topics of dressing and bedtime."

Because he'd kissed her.

"And now I find myself having some difficulty in that area," he stated.

"The books you read..." she began.

"Don't say what to do when she wants to wear the same thing day after day," he said in exasperation. "The kid hates getting dressed, and it takes her forever."

By now Jessica was as curled up as a pretzel, her legs bent beneath her, her navy-blue silk dress in danger of being twisted completely out of shape. Stress. Nerves.

Taking a deep breath, she calmed herself. Standing up, she deliberately reseated herself on the couch, both feet flat on the floor, her dress serenely draped around her legs.

When she spoke, her voice was smooth and collected. "Try laying out her clothes the night before. And let her chose what she wants to wear. At this age they like doing things themselves."

"Hey, I'm all for her being independent and self-sufficient. But I can't stand around all day waiting for her."

His words made Jessica's momentary composure evaporate in an instant. "No, waiting isn't your specialty, is it," she noted tartly.

He certainly hadn't waited for her. He'd probably forgotten about her the moment he'd left town.

"So what should I do about Blue?" Curt demanded. "At this point I'm ready to put her in starched cammies and be done with it."

"Jammies?" she said, unsure she'd heard him correctly.

"Not jammies. Cammies. Camouflage utilities. A uniform. My uniform."

The few times she'd caught sight of him in his camouflage uniform he'd looked only slightly less sexy than when he'd worn those sexy dress blues. Uniform...suddenly it clicked. "Maybe since Blue sees you wearing the same thing to work every day she wants to imitate you and wear the same thing to school."

"I was only kidding about putting her in cammies," Curt said.

"You don't have to put her in cammies. Just wash her outfit every night or get her another one just like it if you can so you could alternate between them. I'm sure she'll grow out of this phase once she's feeling more secure and comfortable about things." Speaking of comfortable, Jessica had once again curled her legs beneath her. Some habits were just too hard to break. "She seems to be reaching out a little more with the other kids at the preschool. Another little girl, Susan, has taken her under her wing. Susan is very outgoing, and she's helping Blue."

"She's the one you paired Blue with that first day, right?"

"That's right." She was surprised he remembered. She'd thought that he hadn't heard a thing she'd said that day because he'd been so eager to dump his daughter and leave. But apparently she might have misjudged him. In that regard, at least.

"There's one more thing..." Curt said.

Her heart skipped and adrenaline raced through her body. If he brought up their kiss, she'd throttle him.

"This coming Sunday is Easter," he continued.

"And I got that flyer you sent home about an Easter Egg hunt on Saturday. Only Blue pasted stickers all over it, and now I can't read any of the details, like time and location."

He wasn't talking about their kiss. So why did she still want to throttle him? He'd probably already forgotten all about it. Fine. She could do the same. She'd focus on school activities and on Blue's progress. She'd treat him the way she would any other parent.

"The Easter Egg hunt takes place at the park just behind the preschool," she replied. "At nine in the morning. The actual hunt begins at quarter after but you need to be there ahead of time as it does get crowded. Do you plan on bringing Blue?" There, her voice sounded perfectly normal. Polite with just the right touch of teacher interest. "I think she'd enjoy it."

"Then I'll bring her," Curt said. "Providing I don't have to dress her up in something frilly for Easter."

"Frilly attire is not required," she assured him.

"Outstanding. We will see you at the aforementioned location at oh-nine hundred hours."

As she hung up the phone, Jessica hoped that by then she'd have rebuilt her defenses where Curt was concerned.

Ah, Saturday morning in the park. Jessica raised her face and basked in the unusual warmth of the sun. The sky was blue, the trees just beginning to show their spring green buds and the sound...well, the sound was just about deafening. The park was already filled with hoards of eager preschoolers clamoring to begin. Last night two of Chicago's weather forecasters had promised rain, but the third had predicted sunny skies.

Jessica was infinitely grateful for the sunshine. Last year rain had pounded the six-foot inflated rabbit that marked the entrance to their egg hunt. Last year the forecasters had predicted sunshine.

More than a dozen staff members and parent volunteers had shown up hours earlier to ensure that the hundreds and hundreds of plastic eggs had been hidden so that three-and four-year-olds could find them. All the staff members, including Jessica, wore yellow T-shirts that said No Yolk, This Is Fun!

Since Sarah Connolly was the preschool director, she had custody of the megaphone, which needed to be used in order to be heard over all the squealing and shouting kids. Two years ago they'd used a thin string to hold the egg hunters at bay, but after one little tyke hadn't been able to wait, he'd started a stampede.

So this year, several of the teacher's aides had linked hands and formed a human chain across the starting line.

Curt arrived precisely at 9:00 a.m. He was wearing his U.S. Marine dress blues, and he looked as impressive as he had that first day he'd walked into her classroom. The other dads' khaki slacks and sport jackets paled in comparison to the military crispness of his attire. The brass buttons gleamed in the sunlight while his white gloves were folded over his belt with knifelike precision.

And holding onto his hand was Blue. Dressed in little girl pink, but minus any frills, she was walking beside her father with a skip in her step and a grin on her face. In her hand was a pink plastic Easter basket.

Jessica's heart lodged in her throat and a bittersweet pain pierced her heart. What would it be like to have a daughter of her own? The longing was so intense that it became an actual physical ache.

She'd become a preschool teacher so that she'd be able to interact with children when they were at their most impressionable age. And her work had helped her come to terms with her situation.

But just when she thought she'd dealt with the fact that she couldn't have children, Curt and his daughter had entered her life and shattered that myth.

"Jessie, Jessie, Jessie!" Seeing her, Blue tugged her father right over. "I'm ready now," she regally stated, like an actress notifying her director that filming could begin.

Gazing down at her, Jessica could see signs of Curt in the obstinate line of Blue's chin and in the depth of her brown eyes. Blue had been anxious all week for the Easter egg hunt to begin. Like most three-year-olds she didn't have any real concept of the passage of time.

"How does this operation proceed?" Curt said. "Are parents supposed to accompany their kids?"

"Most do."

Before Curt could reply, Sarah made her announcement.

"Okay, we're ready to begin now. Let the countdown begin." Sarah's amplified voice carried over the ruckus. "Five, four, three, two, one, go!"

"And they're off," Jessica murmured.

The frantic pursuit of candy and prizes packed away in plastic eggs had begun. Some eggs were "hidden" on the low branches of trees or on the ground, on park benches, even on swings. Others had been placed in loose piles of hay. All were in clear sight and no higher than a little one's eye level.

The preschoolers were racing toward their goals, toting bags, baskets or pails as they scrambled onto the field.

Jessica couldn't help herself. She sought out Blue in the melee. It wasn't hard to find her, she was near Curt, and heaven knew he stood out in the crowd. In addition, they hadn't gotten very far from the starting line where Jessica stood and watched them.

Each time Blue found an egg, she paused to show it to Curt before carefully placing it in the basket. Then she'd stand there and admire it.

While Blue seemed unaware of the other kids running around the park continuing their search, Curt was looking around in alarm. Jessica heard him say, "Hey, the other kids are getting ahead of you. Go get eggs."

Blue just smiled at him.

"Get a move on, kid," he urged her. "You're falling behind. Go on now. Get a move on."

Jessica saw red. Moving swiftly, she joined them to smile reassuringly at Blue. "Blue's doing just fine. Lisa, why don't you take her for a minute?" she asked her teacher's aide. Taking Curt by one arm, she tugged him out of earshot before growling, "Blue's doing fine, but you, Mr. Hotshot Marine, *you're* in big trouble!

"What?" Curt demanded. "Why are you looking at me like that?"

"The purpose of an Easter egg hunt is not to collect more eggs than anyone else."

"Sure it is." He refused to be intimidated by the fact that this was the first Easter egg hunt he'd actually ever participated in. The group foster home hadn't been big on holidays. Not for older kids. And his mother never bothered when he was a real little kid.

But that didn't matter now. The rules of an Easter egg hunt were similar to a search-and-rescue mission. Only in this case, plastic eggs filled with candy were being retrieved. The more, the better. Any blockhead could figure that out.

"The purpose is to have fun," Jessica was saying.

"Fun?" he repeated as if unfamiliar with the term. "Winning *is* fun."

"There are no winners or losers here."

"Oh, I get it." He nodded understandingly. "Because they're all little kids, you don't want to call the others losers."

"They're *not* losers."

"Not in life, no," he clarified. "Just in today's Easter egg hunt."

"Listen, you—" She jabbed him smack-dab in the middle of his fourth shiny brass button. "You're not listening to me."

"Can you get to the point?" His impatient gaze went beyond her shoulder to his daughter, who stood well out of earshot and was showing Lisa a neon-pink egg filled with stickers. "Blue is getting farther behind the longer we stand here jawing."

"She's having fun, Curt. Let her be. Let her find her own way."

His eyes returned to Jessica's face. "What is it you're accusing me of this time?"

"Of being too competitive."

"I'm a Marine. We're supposed to be competitive."

"Not at an Easter egg hunt."

He stiffened. "Excuse me if my manners aren't perfect. This is the first event of this kind I've attended. If we're embarrassing you, this said Marine and his daughter will leave ASAP."

"No." She placed a restraining hand on his arm. "I'm sorry. I didn't mean to imply…"

"What?" he said bitterly. "That I don't fit in with all these yuppie parents? You think I don't already know that?"

She'd hit a nerve, she belatedly realized. "I'm sorry," she repeated. "It's just…you don't have to try so hard to succeed."

"I've already told you…"

"That Marines are trained to succeed. I know." Her voice was soothing, tinged with rueful humor. "But remember what I told you about being flexible?"

"Semper Gumby," he said.

"Excuse me?"

"The Marine motto is Semper Fidelis or Semper Fi. It's Latin for Always Faithful."

The irony wasn't lost on her. Here he was telling her that the Corps he loved so much had a motto that went to the heart of his betrayal with her. For he hadn't been faithful. Not to her. Not even for a short time. And since he'd come back, he hadn't even re-membered her name at first or acknowledged that night in the back seat of his car. He hadn't mentioned their kiss, either. And that had only happened a few days ago.

Let it go, she reminded herself. Don't even go there.

"Marines have the best motto," Curt was saying, "and the best twist on that motto is Semper Gumby. Always Flexible. So if you're asking me if I can be flexible, the answer is yes. On occasion."

She noticed how he kept a watchful eye on Blue, but this time his gaze showed…was that affection? Yes, there was definitely a special light in his eyes as he followed his daughter's progress. It was part awe, part pride, part even fear perhaps. And definitely a big dose of paternal affection. Her irritation melted.

"How are things going with you and Blue?" she asked.

"Fine. You said I should interact with her more so I've got her signed up for a kindergym class at the community center. It starts this afternoon." His voice was filled with enthusiasm. "They have a trampoline and rug-rat-size stuff for her to climb on. That should be good, right?" His gaze returned to Jessica, as if seeking her reassurance.

"I'm certain she'll have a good time. If you don't push her so hard to succeed. The point is to have fun."

"I was told this class would improve her dexterity and motor skills."

"Her motor skills are fine. What she needs more

than anything else right now is love and reassurance. How have things been going on that front?''

He shrugged, absently rubbing one hand down his right thigh.

Curt was such a force to be reckoned with, that more often than not she completely forgot about his limp and the fact that it might be causing him pain.

She knew him better than to show him any sympathy. "Would you mind if we sat down?" Jessica said, nodding toward a nearby park bench. "I've been on the go since early this morning assisting the Easter Bunny in hiding the eggs here."

Joining her, his limp a tad bit more noticeable than usual, he said, "Where *is* the Easter Bunny?" Casting her a suddenly suspicious look, he added, "You better not be harboring any hope that I'm gonna dress in some stupid-looking rabbit costume."

She was trying very hard not to harbor any hopes about him period. But it was hard not to when she saw him working so hard to be a good father to his daughter. Even when he didn't get it right, there was still something about him that was able to score a direct hit on her heart.

She'd tried to be logical and figure out what it was about Curt that got to her. She'd considered the possibility that she was viewing him through the rose-colored glasses of a first love—even if it had been a first love that had gone wrong. But logic didn't seem to play a role in her reaction. And it wasn't just physical, either. Instead it was a much more dangerous thing—an emotional reaction.

Oh, sure, there was plenty of sexual chemistry between them. The kiss at his apartment the other night had proven that without a doubt. But there was more to it than that.

"Jessie?" He waved a hand in front of her face. "You didn't answer my question. So I'll rephrase it as a statement. I am *not* going to dress up like the Easter Bunny."

"I wouldn't dream of having you do so," she replied. "I certainly wouldn't want to ruffle that military dignity of yours."

The truth was that he'd done plenty of volunteer work for Toys for Tots, the Marine Corps designated charity, bringing holiday cheer to underprivileged kids. After all, he'd been there so he knew what it was like not to have anyone care enough about you to get a present for you.

But even at those events, he'd steered clear of the little kids like Blue and focused his attention on the troubled adolescents and teenagers. He'd never felt comfortable around rug-rats, had always felt like he was a bumbling bull in a china store, had always been afraid of the damage he might do.

"I don't ruffle easily," he growled, as much for his own benefit as for hers.

Blue wasn't the only one who ruffled him. Jessie did, too. She still felt as out of reach as ever, despite the way she'd responded to his kiss. He was sure she'd regretted it moments afterward. And so had he. God knew, he had enough on his plate without adding a woman to the mix.

For the past ten years, his life had consisted of a series of moves from one assignment to another, of training and conditioning, of peacekeeping missions and volatile situations. Of owing his loyalty to the

Marines, where the needs of the many outweighed the needs of the few.

His sexual needs had been taken care of over the years by women who knew what they were getting into, who wanted a no-strings affair, who were able to kiss him goodbye without clinging to him, allowing him to walk away without turning back.

But he was no longer footloose. Now he had ties. What would happen when his leg recovered? And he was determined that it would recover, no matter what the medics said. He wasn't going to be stuck training "squids" the rest of his military life. He was a man of action. He wanted to return to his platoon.

And what would happen to Blue if he did return to active duty? He watched her smiling shyly at another child as they searched a low bush for more eggs. Other Marines had kids. But they also had wives who looked after said children while the Marines did their duty for their nation.

Maybe that's what he needed. A wife.

Yeah, right. Like it was something he could just put on his shopping list along with frozen dinners and milk.

Maybe not. But maybe he needed to apply his time-honored and battle-tested leadership traits to the current situation. He'd learned how to improvise, overcome and adapt to get the job done. In this case the job was raising Blue.

A wife would definitely make things easier, for himself and for Blue. He wasn't being totally selfish here. The little girl could use some feminine influence for all that kissing and cuddling emotional stuff.

Jessie was sure good at it. And she'd be a great

mom, too. She'd probably make a good wife, too, albeit a bossy one.

Jessie as *his* wife. Now there was a concept.

Shaking his head, Curt had to laugh. Somehow he couldn't see her going along with his plans.

Yeah, she'd kissed him. And she'd been damn good at it, too. But he was still the bad boy, and she was still Jessie the Brain. Why would she want to get involved with a gimpy Marine? It wasn't as though he had much to offer her.

For the time being, he'd just have to manage things one day at a time. For the next month at least, he'd still be regaining the use of his leg. After that point, he'd have to see what developed.

Chapter Six

"Where do you find the time?" Lisa, her teaching assistant, asked Jessica early Wednesday morning before the kids arrived. "You're always here before anyone else and you stay longer afterward as well. Where do you find the time to have a life?"

"What life?" Jessica retorted, only half kidding.

The truth was that Jessica devoted most of her time to her job, and it seemed to have gotten worse lately. Which was fine by her. The extra hours spent working prevented her from thinking too much about things she shouldn't. Like Curt. Or the fact that Trevor hadn't called back since their date last week. No surprise there.

Actually Trevor wasn't the issue here. It was Curt. After spending much of Saturday with him at the Easter Egg hunt, she could feel herself softening toward him. Nervous at that realization, she'd thrown herself into her work even more so than usual the past few days.

Looking around her room, Jessica noted with pride that the extra time she'd put in showed. To her own eyes if to no one else's. She was a strong believer in the way that one's physical surroundings affected how people feel. It was one of the reasons her own home followed a streamlined format, with just a few choice pieces of furniture in each room.

Here at work, the building had been completely renovated into four large spaces for four classrooms and one smaller area for the office. Two of the areas were reserved for morning and afternoon preschool sessions, while the others two were for longer day care situations. Within her classroom were clearly defined and well-equipped interest areas designed to promote a child's ability to learn through play.

In the front corner was the so-called "house" corner where the children could play house, or store, or a variety of roles. Today she'd come in early to set it up as a grocery store complete with appropriate props like a counter, play money and shelves with preschooler-size cans and artificial fruits and vegetables for sale.

In the back corner were the table toys, with a large table to spread out puzzles and games that encouraged kids to match, sort and make patterns.

Beside that was what Jessica ruefully referred to as Water Beach. A nearby sink provided the water while the large sandbox provided the sand. Here the kids did everything from sifting sand to water play, exploring why some objects sink and others float. Plenty of plastic measuring cups, sifters and strainers were available in this section.

A safe distance away from that was the reading corner where a large selection of books were stacked in cubbyholes and baskets, easily accessible for small hands to pull out and look through. Beside that was the computer and art corner.

In fact, she'd just changed the art display of the children's work to show the brightly colored crayon drawings they'd made of their experiences at Saturday's Easter Egg hunt.

She put in the extra time and effort because she wanted the kids to all know that they were important and valued.

"The new display looks great," Lisa was saying. "You've got a real eye for that sort of thing. When I put the pictures up they look like a jumbled mess. But when you do it, each one takes on a life of its own."

"Thanks, but we're a team here. I couldn't do it without you." Lisa and the other assistant, Tawanna, each supervised a group of four or five kids at one of the play stations while Jessica worked with them at another. That way each child got a variety of experiences.

But it did require a great deal of organization. The schedule was one even a Marine like Curt would be proud of.

Her day might seem like a jumble of removing coats, telling stories, singing songs, eating snacks and playing on swings and in sandboxes—but it had to have a balance of active and quiet times, large group actives and small group interaction as well as indoor and outdoor play. However, Jessica was flexible enough so that if something was especially successful there was no reason to stop it just because her schedule stated it was time to do something else.

Semper Gumby. Curt's words about being flexible came back to her as so many of his words seemed to lately. And not just his words. There was still that kiss that neither one of them had mentioned.

"So what's on the agenda today?" Lisa asked, her long dark hair swinging around her shoulders as she leaned down to gently shove a puzzle box back into place. The shelves were neat and uncluttered so that the kids weren't overwhelmed and were easily able to seek out and find what they wanted.

"Today is sand castle building day, among other things," Jessica replied.

Lisa grinned. "My favorite."

"Let's just pray they don't all want to build sand castles at the same time."

While some programs had the children rotating from one activity to another at a signal from the teacher, here the children had a say in what they wanted to do next.

"I think shopping could provide some strong competition," Lisa said.

"And then we've got those easels set up in the art corner," Jessica added. "I think there's plenty to tempt them."

"Speaking of tempting," Lisa said, "did you notice that Blue's dad came to the Easter Egg hunt in his dress blues uniform?"

"He was hard to miss."

"He sure was. I noticed him that first day when he

dropped off Blue. He wore the same uniform then.''
Lisa sighed and rolled her gorgeous almond-shaped
eyes the way only a nineteen-year-old could. There
were times when Jessica felt decades older than her
Asian-American assistant. When she'd made love
with Curt, Jessica had been only a year younger than
Lisa. She'd still had stars in her eyes. That was no
longer the case.

"I thought you were going in for the academic type
these days," Jessica reminded her.

Lisa's dark eyes were dreamy as she sighed again.
"There's just something about a man in uniform."

Especially if that man was Curt.

It was ridiculous of her to feel a sting of jealousy
just because Lisa, who was younger and much prettier, happened to notice Curt, who probably went in
for younger prettier women rather than quiet preschool teachers who couldn't have children.

There it was again, that label attached to her iden-
tity.

She knew it wasn't Curt's fault that her doubts and
insecurities had returned en masse. This was a private
battle and one she'd have to fight on her own. But it
did serve to prove how vulnerable she was where Curt
was concerned.

"Were you two girlfriends talking about that fine,
fine Marine?" Tawanna demanded as she joined
them. At fifty, with four grandchildren of her own,
Tawanna had a lusty passion for life that Jessica ad-
mired. With her short dark hair and flawless ebony
complexion, Tawanna looked younger than her age.
A self-proclaimed "large" woman and proud of it,
she delighted in wearing brilliant colors. Today she'd

selected a flowing caftan in lemon yellow and purple. "Back up and tell me what I missed."

"You missed nothing," Jessica maintained. "Did you bring in those pictures of your new granddaughter like you promised?"

Hands on her ample hips, Tawanna fixed her with a reprimanding stare. "If you think you can distract me by talking about my new grandbaby, let me tell you right now..." She broke into a huge smile. "You're right."

A moment later she whipped out an orange packet of photographs and proceeded to give a colorful interpretation of each shot. By the time she was finished, the children were beginning to arrive.

Engrossed with quickly putting the finishing touches on the store setup, Jessica didn't see Curt when he dropped off Blue. He'd made a point lately of bringing himself to Jessica's attention as he strode into a room that seemed to shrink with the power of his presence.

Even the kids noticed it. And him. Every time class hellion Brian saw Curt, he asked him where his tank was.

But this morning Blue was the one clamoring for Jessica's attention. "Jessie, Jessie, Jessie!"

The little girl raced toward her for her morning hug, staying still a brief moment before backing off with a shy smile. "Jessie come see me at kinder-gym!"

Blue stood there, her big brown eyes staring at her so intently, as she rocked slightly from side to side as if unable to contain her nervous excitement.

There were plenty of other things Jessica should be

doing this Saturday. The wash was piling up, there was junk mail that needed sorting and her fridge was almost empty while her grocery list was an arm long.

But the bottom line was that Jessica simply didn't have the heart to disappoint a little girl who'd already had more than her fair share of hard knocks. The errands and housework would have to wait.

"Okay. I'll be there."

"Promise?" Blue insisted.

"I promise."

And so it was that Jessica found herself walking into the local community center on Saturday afternoon to join a bunch of other parents seated in one corner of the gymnasium. She hadn't told Curt she was coming and didn't know if Blue had alerted him. The little girl had talked of little else for the remainder of the week, and she waved at Jessica the second she saw her.

"Your little girl is adorable," the woman seated beside her said. "I've got five boys. I keep hoping for a girl.

Your little girl. The words fell on top of Jessica like a load of bricks, bruising her with their forbidden promise.

"She's not mine," Jessica curtly replied, her voice sounding rudely abrupt even to her own ears.

The other woman was clearly flustered. "Oh, I'm sorry. I just thought..."

"That's okay," Jessica said, but it wasn't. How could it be? When she wished with all her heart that Blue was hers.

She would have gotten up and left but for the fact that Blue looked up and waved at her again, this time shouting, "Watch me, watch me!" She did a tumbling routine that had more sheer joy than coordination.

Meanwhile Curt, with clipboard in hand, was studying his daughter as critically as any Olympic judge. Jessica half expected him to hold up score cards afterward. When would he learn?

Curt could feel Jessica's disapproval even from halfway across the gymnasium and briefly wondered what he could possibly have done wrong this time. He hadn't used the term winners or losers at all today. Instead he was teaching his daughter how to improve her tumbling routine. What harm could there possibly be in that?

"Okay," he told her, "now focus, Blue. You are...?"

"A Marine kid," she replied, just as he'd taught her to.

"Who?" he prompted her.

"Never gives up. And is three. I can do it myself," she told him, wiggling to be set free so she could attack the padded blue floor mat with another series of wobbly somersaults.

Holding on to her and staring her in the eye, Curt said, "You need to have a plan. Remember the Six *P*'s Rule?"

She blinked at him guilelessly. "Don't hafta pee."

Curt refused to blush. A Marine never blushed. "I'm talking about the letter *P*. Proper Prior Prevention Prevents Poor Performance." This was something he'd picked up way back in Intro to Survival Training, but Curt saw no reason why it shouldn't work in this situation as well. "See how that boy over there balances so well? That's what you're aiming for, short-stuff. That's your goal. Do you read me?''

Instead of saluting, she just grinned and patted him on the cheek before slipping away.

"Okay, moms and dads," the instructor was saying. "It's time to switch apparatus."

"I don't like aspar-gus," Blue told her father with a frown. "It's long and green."

"She said apparatus, not asparagus," Curt assured her. "Now remember our game plan." He waved his clipboard at her as if hoping she'd be able to decipher the notes and diagrams he'd scribbled. Glancing down at them himself, he realized they were more complicated than most NFL teams game books. Like a general on a campaign, he'd drawn up an intricate set of battle plans.

Meanwhile his daughter was skipping toward the padded mat as if she didn't have a care in the world.

"Watch me!" she yelled over the voices of the other kids in the class.

In the midst of her somersault she wavered like a drunk, her little fanny aimed at the ceiling, but she recovered enough to make it through without completely tipping over.

As Curt cheered his approval, Blue stood up and grinned...only to trip over her own two feet.

To her credit, she didn't cry after falling down but got right up and kept going into her next tumbling routine.

"Did you see that?" Curt turned to ask Jessica, who'd come to join him. "She didn't quit, but kept on going."

"Yes, I saw. I also saw you coaching her."

"There some law against that?"

"No." Looking down at his clipboard, she added, "Providing you're not expecting her to do too much."

"You set low goals and you never reach the heights."

As he went to rejoin his daughter, Jessica remembered the heights she'd reached with Curt in the back of his Mustang.

Her goals had been very lofty at the time. She'd wanted him to love her. She'd wanted him to take her away and give her happiness. She'd wanted to give him children.

But another woman had done that for him. Had he loved Blue's mother? He'd shown no signs of grieving, but then he always kept his emotions under a tight lid. She'd heard remorse in his voice when he spoke of Gloria, but nothing else.

How pitiful arc you? her inner voice scoffed. Here you are scrambling after crumbs that Curt hadn't loved Gloria even if she'd borne his child. He should have loved her. Blue deserved two parents who loved her. Every child did.

But Jessica knew all too well that the reality was quite different. The important thing was having someone who loved you.

Could Curt be that someone for Blue, be what she needed in a parent?

He was showing signs of improvement, of being more open than he had been in the beginning. And there was no mistaking the pride on his face when he'd watched Blue go through her tumbling routine. He was wearing jeans and a T-shirt, yet he still managed to stand out from the other dads. And she couldn't blame it on the U.S. Marine Corps T-shirt he was wearing, despite the fact that it fit him to perfection and drew attention to his broad shoulders and muscular arms.

No, it wasn't the uniform. It had never been the uniform. It was Curt.

He was getting to her. Bit by bit.

"Thanks for coming with us for an early dinner," Curt said as he held the door to Dino's open for Jessica.

Since leaving the kindergym session at the nearby community center, Blue had insisted on holding on to Jessica's hand as well as her father's. So Jessica found herself tethered to Curt, with a child providing the link. It was hard not to be affected by the metaphor here. Or not to be affected by the man and his child.

In the three weeks since he'd walked into her preschool classroom, he'd changed in some ways and remained stubbornly the same in others. He was still a study of contrasts. The rigidity of his cropped dark hair remained at war with the sensual fullness of his mouth and the heated intensity of his brown eyes. He'd still had the ability to consume her with a single glance. That much hadn't changed.

But there were differences. The recent scar that formed a ragged line along his jaw was beginning to heal. He seemed more at ease with her and with Blue.

And Blue had changed as well. No longer was she the frightened little girl, her brown hair tied up into two lopsided pigtails, who'd stood nervously beside Curt, close enough to touch him but not doing so.

The beat-up lime-green thin jacket she'd worn that day had since been replaced with a cheerful yellow rain slicker that kept today's rainy weather at bay.

Pausing near the open door, Blue pointed up before telling Jessica and Curt, "The sky is crying. My mommy lives there in the sky. In heaven. Is she crying, too?"

Chapter Seven

Curt gave Jessica a bewildered look that let her know he was still uncertain about how to deal with the subject of Gloria's death. That he revealed even that much was a big step. Not long ago he would have responded with a steely-eyed expression that rejected any emotion. Yes, he was coming around, slowly but surely.

Then Blue went on to ask, "Can you somersault when you get dead?"

Now Curt's expression was tinged with panic. Since Curt was so uncomfortable with the subject during Daddy Boot Camp, Jessica had only had time to caution him not to tell Blue that death was like sleeping, because that would make the little girl afraid to fall asleep. She hadn't had gone on to tell him what to say. But at the moment he looked incapable of speaking at all.

"If you're in heaven, I don't see why you couldn't

GET FREE BOOKS and a FREE GIFT
WHEN YOU PLAY THE...

SLOT MACHINE GAME!

Just scratch off the silver box with a coin. Then check below to see the gifts you get!

YES! I have scratched off the silver box. Please send me the 2 free books and gift for which I qualify. I understand I am under no obligation to purchase any books, as explained on the back of this card.

315 SDL C4GU

215 SDL C4GQ
(S-R-OS-09/00)

NAME (PLEASE PRINT CLEARLY)

ADDRESS

APT.#   CITY

STATE/PROV.   ZIP/POSTAL CODE

7	7	7	**Worth TWO FREE BOOKS plus a BONUS Mystery Gift!**
			Worth TWO FREE BOOKS!
			Worth ONE FREE BOOK!
			TRY AGAIN!

Offer limited to one per household and not valid to current Silhouette Romance® subscribers. All orders subject to approval.

© 2000 HARLEQUIN ENTERPRISES LTD. ® and TM are trademarks owned by Harlequin Books S.A. used under license.

DETACH AND MAIL CARD TODAY!

The Silhouette Reader Service™ — Here's how it works:

Accepting your 2 free books and gift places you under no obligation to buy anything. You may keep the books and gift and return the shipping statement marked "cancel." If you do not cancel, about a month later we'll send you 6 additional novels and bill you just $2.90 each in the U.S., or $3.25 each in Canada, plus 25¢ shipping & handling per book and applicable taxes if any.* That's the complete price and — compared to cover prices of $3.50 each in the U.S. and $3.99 each in Canada — it's quite a bargain! You may cancel at any time, but if you choose to continue, every month we'll send you 6 more books, which you may either purchase at the discount price or return to us and cancel your subscription.

*Terms and prices subject to change without notice. Sales tax applicable in N.Y. Canadian residents will be charged applicable provincial taxes and GST.

do somersaults there," Jessica replied, smoothing back Blue's damp hair from her face.

"Will Tawanna get dead?" Blue said.

Squeezing the little girl's hand, Jessica replied, "Not for a long time hopefully."

Turning away from Jessica, Blue intently stared up at her father. "Will you get dead, Daddy?"

Curt stood there, frozen, unable to use the old line that Marines never die, they just go to hell and re-group.

"Everybody dies sometime," he said, his voice sounding rusty even to his own ears. Clearing his throat, he added, "But I plan on being around for a very long time. Until you're at least as old as I am."

"Everybody dies?" Blue repeated, her eyes going as big as saucers. "Even the Easter Bunny?"

"Uh, well, I'm no expert on the Easter Bunny," Curt replied, backpedaling. "Jessie knows more about that stuff than I do."

"You folks need a booster seat?" Emily, a long-time waitress interrupted them to ask. Bending down to Blue, she said, "Well, hi there, sweet pea."

Emily had been working at Dino's for as long as Jessica could remember. She usually only worked the weekday afternoon shift, so Jessica didn't get to see her that often anymore. The sixty-something waitress was known for her outgoing personality and flamboyant earrings. Today the earrings were dangling red cherries that bobbed around her face as spoke to Blue. "Aren't you just the cutest thing."

"No," Blue said. "G.I. Joe is cuter than me."

To give him credit, Curt didn't immediately correct her by saying that the military action figure wasn't cute. Instead he firmly stated, "No one is cuter than my daughter."

Blue beamed. Just beamed.

Jessica wanted to reach out and hug Curt. She wished she had the words to tell him how important this moment was, how much a little girl needed her father's love and approval.

Not having received either from her own father, Jessica knew firsthand how you could spend a lifetime longing for something you never had. First it had been her father's love, then it had been Curt's love, and then it had been a child's love. And while the children in her classes loved her while they were with her, they moved on. The way Curt had moved on. Another group of children came in at the preschool, and the process began again. But none of the children were hers.

Other men had come into her life. But none of them were the love of her life. None of them were meant to be hers.

Standing there looking at Curt, she wondered how her life and his would have been different if he had loved her the way she'd loved him all those years ago.

Jessica knew there was no point in living in the past. She also knew that new beginnings were as tenuous as a seedling first breaking through the soil, easily crushed by forces outside its own control. But with enough sunshine and water it could grow into something as sturdy as an oak tree.

She had no idea if what she had with Curt was something that could grow beyond the seedling stage.

But she was curious enough to stay for now and find out.

"I can't believe this place is still here," Curt said as he helped Blue into the plastic booster seat Emily had placed at a table near the front window. "Do they still serve great cheeseburgers and curly fries?"

"Yes, they do." Jessica reached for the chair across from him, but before she could pull it out he was there to do it for her. "Thanks." After sitting down, she could feel his warm breath on her nape as he leaned closer to gently scoot the chair in. A little courtesy that made her senses hum.

"I used to imagine I was eating one of those burgers instead of an MRE," he admitted, before returning to his side of the table.

"A what?"

"Meal ready to eat."

She wrinkled her nose. "Doesn't sound very appetizing."

"The beef frankfurters and beans aren't bad when you're out in the field. But then you don't join the Marines for the food."

"Why did you join?" She'd been wanting to ask him that question for some time.

"To see the world."

She had the feeling he wasn't telling her the entire story but she didn't challenge his answer. "And have you done that?"

"I've participated in several joint service and training operations in Japan, South Korea and the Philippines, as well as real world contingency crisis situations in the Middle East and most recently Bosnia."

"Is that where you were wounded?"

"I was wounded in my right thigh," he dryly replied.

Just thinking about his thighs made Jessica blush. Reaching for her iced water, she gulped the cold liquid and prayed he wouldn't notice her bright red cheeks.

Little chance of that. But to her relief, he made no comment. Unfortunately Blue did.

"Jessie's face is red."

"Because I'm hot. It's warm in here." She tugged on the open collar of her pink blouse. "Don't you think so?"

Curt thought she should continue whatever she was doing with her shirt because it allowed him to get brief glimpses of her shadowy cleavage. Now *he* was the one getting hot.

"So you joined the Marines to travel," she was saying. "It sounds like you've done a great deal of that over the past ten years. That's why you've stayed in the Marine Corps?"

"I stay because of the camaraderie. A group of kids all from different parts of the country—some rich, most not, some educated, some not—train together. When you head out on an operation and leave the U.S., you realize that this is for real and that you can't screw up. Your biggest fear is of making a mistake and causing another Marine to get hurt. Those guys are my family."

"Blue is your family now," she reminded him.

"I know that."

Did he? His voice had been so filled with emotion when he talked about the Marines. It was obvious he loved the life.

She also wondered if his biggest parenting fear was making a mistake and causing his daughter to get hurt. Asking him outright wouldn't get her anywhere. She'd have to finagle the answer out of him.

"That must be a great deal of pressure and responsibility, feeling that you have to be perfect or someone could get hurt."

He shrugged. "Crisis situations are opportunities for someone to get hurt. You just work to make sure it's not anyone in your command."

"Or yourself," she added. "Unless you're saying that you'd put your troops' welfare above your own?"

"Marines aren't troops." He sounded insulted. "We're Marines. With a capital *M*."

"Fine." The man was as prickly as a hedgehog. Not that a Marine would approve of being likened to a hedgehog. He'd have to be as prickly as a...a hand grenade. "But you haven't answered my question."

"As their commanding officer it's my job to make sure they get out safely, and in order to accomplish that job I have to stay alive."

He was tap-dancing around the question. She had to smile at that mental image. A Marine tap-dancing. Another no-no. "And if someone makes a mistake?"

"To err may be human and to forgive divine." He gave her a solemn look belied by the gleam in his brown eyes. "However, neither is Marine Corps Policy."

"Which is why Marine Corps Policy can't be applied to parenthood," she replied.

"I don't see why it couldn't be adapted for parenthood."

"Because you're bound to make mistakes and the best you can hope for is to learn from them."

He nodded and said, "Like stickers."

She blinked at him in confusion. "Excuse me?"

"I learned not to give stickers to short-stuff here." He tilted his head in Blue's direction, who was coloring with the crayons and paper Emily had given her. "Because she has a tendency to put them all over my stuff. She even stuck them on the soles of my shoes. But she knows not to do that anymore."

"Look, Daddy, look! Look what I made!" She waved her picture at him, almost knocking over his glass of water in the process.

"Careful there, short-stuff," he said, but his voice lacked the drill sergeant bite it had had when he'd first gotten custody of Blue. "Let's see what you've got here." He bent his head close to his daughter to get a good look at her drawing.

"Me," Blue said, pointing to the smaller of the blobs. "Daddy and Jessie."

"We make a nice couple," Curt told Jessica as he held up the drawing for her approval. They looked like a couple of bowling balls with feet to him. But hey, he was no art critic. And if his kid drew it, then it was the best drawing this side of the Chicago Art Institute.

"You folks ready to order?" Emily asked.

"Maybe I should cut back on the fries." Curt nodded at the drawing he still held before patting his flat stomach.

"I don't think you have anything to worry about," Jessica dryly assured him. She on the other hand, had plenty to worry about. Not in the tummy department. But in the "Curt" department.

After ordering, Curt let Blue tell him the story of what she was drawing now, which had something to do with the Easter Bunny and G.I. Joe. Jessica was content to sit back and watch them. It gave her pleasure to see how well Curt was interacting with Blue.

Okay, so it gave her pleasure just looking at Curt period. But it also made her feel good to see that he was making great strides in his parenting skills. Of course he couldn't resist giving Blue one or two instructions on how to improve her drawing, his version of a "color within the lines" speech. But when Blue ignored him, he let her do her own thing.

Once the food arrived, talking was abandoned in favor of taking mouthwatering bites of cheeseburger topped with fresh tomatoes and lettuce. Blue got a hot dog from the kiddy menu.

"Mmm," Curt mumbled.

"No talking with mouth full," Blue reprimanded him, patting his arm as a reminder.

"Mmm" was all Curt said, his eyes still closed in ecstasy.

Blue reached over to snitch one of his French fries, only to cry out as she bit into the too hot center.

"Ow!" Her big brown eyes swam with tears that rapidly ran down her face.

Curt's eyes snapped open to stare at his daughter with concern. "What happened?"

"Here, Blue, sip some cold water," Jessica said, holding the glass to Blue's lips while smoothing the hair back from her face with a loving hand. She then answered Curt's question. "She took one of your fries and burned her mouth.'' Returning her attention to Blue, she said, ''It's okay, sweetie. You'll be okay.''

Curt watched in amazement and relief as his daughter's tears quickly evaporated. He'd closed his eyes just for a second and Blue had hurt herself. He felt that wave of guilt, just as he had that first week when Blue had gone to bed with her shoes still on. What made him think he'd ever master this parenting stuff? Just when he thought he was making progress, something happened to set him back on his butt and teach him yet again that he wasn't father material.

A Marine never gives up. So he had setbacks. They were bound to occur. He had to learn from them and move on.

One thing he'd learned was how good Jessica was with Blue.

''You're good with kids,'' he noted quietly.

She shrugged off his words. ''It's my job.''

''It's more than a job,'' Curt said in the voice of one who knew what it was like to have a calling rather than just filling time with a job.

Their eyes met. No words were spoken but something special was shared. The visual exchange had a disturbing effect on her metabolism, making her heart beat faster, making her want...him. The noisy restaurant seemed to fade into the background and time stood still, as she simply gazed into the heated intensity of his brown eyes.

The sound of Blue's fork clattering on the floor shattered the moment. Blinking, Jessica pulled herself away from the powerful bond forged between herself and Curt by nothing more than a mere look. Ah, but what a look it had been!

Automatically reaching down to pick up the cutlery, Jessica smiled at Blue who was tugging on her tongue and trying to look down at it at the same time. "Does your mouth still hurt, sweetie?"

Blue nodded. She stopped her tongue-tugging when Curt suggested ordering some ice cream. Pointing at a picture on the kid's activity place mat, she said, "How come kitties purr and we don't?"

"Because we're not kitties," Jessica replied.

Blue nodded again, as if satisfied with that answer, before suddenly leaning over to rest her head on Jessica's shoulder. "I love you," she said, gazing up at her with a smile that was pure gold.

It wasn't the first time one of her preschoolers had told her that. She'd loved them all back while managing to keep a certain emotional distance. Because the kids moved on. She'd trained herself to accept this, to enjoy them while they were with her and put them out of her mind when they weren't. Sometimes that was harder to do than others. But never had it become as impossible as it was with Blue.

And it wasn't merely because the little girl was Curt's daughter. It wasn't simply because the little girl had so tragically lost her own mother. No, it was just Blue.

"I love you, too," Jessica whispered, running her fingers through Blue's baby fine hair.

The moment the ice cream arrived, Blue straightened and focused all her attention on the dessert. Jessica didn't find it that easy to dismiss her own turbulent emotions.

After spurning her attempts to pay for her own meal and insisting on paying the entire bill himself,

Curt bundled the now tired-looking Blue back into her yellow rain slicker with military efficiency. The fact that the little one didn't protest was a clear indication that she was sleepy.

Once they were all outside the restaurant, Curt offered to walk Jessica home.

"No, that's okay," Jessica quickly replied. "I only live a few blocks away. And Blue is ready to fall asleep." Looking closer, she said, "I think she already has fallen asleep." The sight of the little girl's cheek resting against Curt's shoulder made Jessica's heart melt.

Oh, yeah, Curt and his daughter were getting to her, all right. Big time.

It was too late to protect herself. Too late to tell herself she should have kept her distance. All she could do now was pray that she'd be strong enough to say goodbye when the time came for Curt and Blue to move on.

"What's the big deal?" Curt demanded of his reflection in the bathroom mirror. "Just pick up the phone and call her. What?" he mocked himself. "You can handle grenade launchers and you're afraid of a cute preschool teacher?"

Marching into the bedroom, he grabbed for the portable phone. She answered on the fourth ring. "Hello?"

"Are you okay?" he demanded. "You sound kind of breathless."

"I just got out of the shower."

Weak at the knees, he sank onto his bed and closed his eyes, imagining her standing on the other end of the line holding the phone in one hand and a towel in the other. She wasn't the type to go traipsing around the house in the nude. No, she'd have grabbed a towel. But she might not have had time to wrap it around herself very well and it might not cover very much. It certainly wouldn't cover all of her long legs. Or the gentle curve of her breasts.

An image flashed into his mind of a younger Jessie, her long honey-blond hair cascading around her bare shoulders as she hovered above him in the semidarkness. Her shy smile as she ran her hands over his chest, the rosy tip of her nipples exposed to his view between the silken strands of her hair as she moved...

He groaned. It seemed so real, as if it were a real memory of a time gone by.

"Is something wrong?" she asked him. "Is it Blue? Is something wrong with Blue?"

"No." He was the one who was in danger of cardiac arrest. The thought of her in nothing but water droplets and a towel was enough to make his heart stop, not to mention that disturbingly erotic flashback. He tried to swallow. "No, Blue is fine. She's dancing."

"You called me to tell me that Blue's dancing?"

Hearing the amusement in Jessie's voice, he marshaled his thoughts in order. "In a program. They've got this ballet thing going in conjunction with the kindergym operation. She'll be on stage this Sunday afternoon, providing I can get her in the stupid outfit. Do you have any idea how hard it is to put tights on kids?"

"Yes, actually I do," she wryly assured him.

"Well, I had no idea. I know advanced weapon

systems that require less maneuvering. And can deploy much faster, too.''

"So you want me there to help you get Blue dressed?''

"Negative. I can get her dressed.'' Or die trying. "She and I would both like you in the audience to watch her perform. Well, actually she's not doing much more than standing on tiptoe, putting her hands over her head and moving across the stage. But hey, Julia Roberts probably started her stage career that way, too.''

"I can tell that once again you've got big plans for Blue,'' she mocked him.

"Are you going to lecture me again?'' he demanded.

"Are you going to listen this time?'' she replied.

"I always listen, Jessie.'' His voice turned warm and husky. "But I pay attention to your actions even more. Like when you kissed me.''

He heard her startled gasp.

Then she firmly said, "I think we should forget that kiss.''

"I'm going to have to decline that request.''

"It wasn't a request,'' she shot back, "it was an order.''

"We're no longer in Daddy Boot Camp. So you're no longer in a position to be giving me orders.'' He came up with a few other positions he'd sure like her to be in, on this bed with him, her bare body beneath his...

His hot fantasy was interrupted by the sound of her blowing a raspberry at him over the phone line.

"I'll come watch Blue dance," she told him. "But don't go getting any other ideas, Mr. Macho Marine."

Not get ideas? About her? Impossible! She might as well tell him to take up flower arranging.

He would have told her so, but the dial tone informed him that she'd already hung up.

The community center auditorium was crowded by the time Jessica arrived. She ran into a few parents of children who'd been in her classes in the past and paused to exchange a few words with them. Curt had told her to save him a seat, so when she found two aisle seats about halfway to the stage, she snagged them. He joined her just as the lights went down and the slightly crooked stage curtain parted.

"Sorry to be late." He leaned close to whisper in her ear. "There was a problem with Blue's tights. She peeled them off twice, so she and I had a little talk. I think everything is under control now."

Her pulse certainly wasn't under control, not with his warm breath brushing against her skin. There was an unexpected intimacy in sitting so close to him in the darkness. He was wearing his dress blues uniform, and even though it was only the third time she'd ever seen him in it, she still got a little weak at the knees. Okay, more than a little, she corrected herself as a ripple of sensual excitement slid up her spine.

"Look, there she is!" Curt's voice was excited, but it was caused by his daughter's dancing debut, not by his closeness to Jessica.

Looking up at the stage, she saw that Blue had indeed made her appearance near the end of a line of half a dozen preschoolers, all decked out as little ballerinas—complete with pink leotards, white tutus and little flower headbands in their hair. They slowly made their way from one end of the stage to the other accompanied by the sound of Tchaikovsky's "The Waltz of the Flowers."

The scene was so perfect.

Then disaster struck as Blue kicked her leg like a Radio City Hall Rockette, her ballet-shoe clad foot smacking into the behind of the little girl in front of her...who fell into the girl in front of her.

One by one, like a row of rapidly tumbling dominoes, the baby ballerinas all went sprawling across the stage.

Bedlam broke out as startled little girls started wailing and concerned parents started shouting. The only one left standing on stage was Blue, who proudly smiled and waved at Curt.

As the houselights quickly came on, and a voice over the loudspeaker assured the audience that no one was hurt, Jessica turned to Curt in confusion. "Why would Blue do something like that?"

The guilty look on his face told her that he knew the reason.

"What did you do this time?" she demanded.

"I should go see if Blue is okay," he said, propping his hand on the back of his seat to propel himself upward without putting too much weight on his injured leg.

"Wait a minute."

For a man with a limp, he was suddenly moving very quickly. As if he had something or someone he was trying to escape. "Not so fast," she said, hurrying after him to keep up. She reached him in the small outer lobby. "What did you do? I saw the look on your face. I know that you did or said something that precipitated her actions."

"Okay, I may have said something about going out there and kicking some butts, but I didn't mean for her to take that literally."

"She's three, Curt. She takes everything literally."

"I know that," he said defensively.

"If you know that then why did you say what you did? You did it because it's always about coming out on top with you, isn't it. Always about winning." Her voice rose angrily.

Noticing the attention they were getting, Curt tugged her into the tiny coatroom for a moment and closed the door. "Would you just calm down a minute...."

"No, I won't calm down," she replied, yanking her arm away from his clasp. "I don't even know why I bother talking to you. You don't pay attention to anything I say!"

"That's not true."

"It's absolutely true," she said, interrupting him, so furious with him she could hardly see straight. "You ignore me, just the way you ignored me all those years ago when you came back from boot camp after we'd made love. It was always about winning with you, wasn't it? Even back then."

Stunned, he stared at her. "We made love?"

Chapter Eight

"Yes, we made love," Jessica said, so upset now that she was actually shaking. "Maybe it was just sex for you, but it was my first time—"

"Hold on a minute." Curt held up his hand, his expression taut. "Let me get this straight. You and I made love? When? Where?"

"In your car the night before you left to join the Marines. Obviously it was a memorable and life-altering experience for you," she noted with mocking bitterness.

"I had too much to drink that night," he acknowledged. "The next morning my memory was blurry."

"Oh, spare me the excuses."

"I'm not making excuses, I'm telling you the truth. I didn't remember. Not because it wasn't memorable. I have been getting these mental images, but I thought...well, I never thought they were real." They seemed too good to be real. Her long honey-colored hair falling over him like a heavenly Victoria's Secret angel, her body wrapped around his. He'd never dreamed that he'd gone all the way with her, that she'd ever have let him. Well, he'd dreamed, yeah, but he never thought it could ever have happened.

"Oh, it was real all right," she said. "Real enough that I thought I was pregnant. I even took one of those home pregnancy tests. It came out positive. I was going to tell you that when you came home, but you never even contacted me to let me know you were home. And when I did see you, you ignored me."

The blood drained from his face. "You were pregnant?"

Her lips trembled and she shook her head. "As it turned out the test results were inaccurate. There was no baby. There never will be a baby. Not for me." Holding back a sob, she shoved past him.

"Jessie, wait!" He reached for her, but the tortured look in her eyes stopped him.

"I can't do this," she said, her voice shaking with emotion.

"Daddy!" Blue wailed from farther down the hallway. *"Daddy!"*

"Go see to your daughter and leave me alone!" Backing away from him, Jessica turned and fled.

Laundry. Jessica was going to do the laundry and not think about how she'd made a fool of herself in front of Curt.

An hour after the disastrous event, the tears had stopped and the regret had set in.

What had she been thinking? Why did she have to

go and bring up the past? Had she honestly thought that he'd say something to make her feel better?

He hadn't. Telling her he couldn't remember that night at all...well, that just seemed to sum it all up. She was completely forgettable.

Just as she was forgettable by her own father, who never seemed to see her. No matter how much she tried to please him, he never noticed. Which was why Curt's behavior had hurt all the more.

When would she learn? Was she doomed to love men who couldn't love her in return? Was she so unlovable?

Biting her bottom lip, she decided she'd had enough of this gloomy soul-searching. No more. Narrowing her eyes and willing the tears away, she instead focused her attention on the pile of dirty clothes before her. No more thinking about the past and about Curt.

She was hereby declaring this to be a Curt-free zone. No thoughts of Curt were allowed in her tiny laundry room. In fact, she'd declare her entire condo to be a Curt-free zone.

Yes, she liked that idea.

Instead she'd think about sorting whites from colors. She'd remember that her rayon pants needed to be line-dried and not tossed in the dryer. This was something she could do. Get something accomplished. Wash laundry, toss in dryer, remove and fold. Repeat with the next load.

Two hours later there was nothing left to wash. She'd even laundered two tablecloths that hadn't needed it. Which left her with...the closet. She'd been meaning to clean out her bedroom closet. After paus-

ing long enough to order a pizza to be delivered—all
that washing had made her hungry and it was almost
dinnertime—she undertook the project with the determination of a Marine.

No, not a Marine. Marines were a pain in the behind.

As if on cue, the phone rang.

It was him. She just knew it. Jessica eyed the white
cordless telephone on her bedside table with narrowed
eyes. Amy had gone camping in Wisconsin for the
weekend, so it wasn't her calling. No, it was definitely
Curt. She could tell just by the way the phone was
ringing, even the sound seemed to reflect his own
impatient dominance.

Sure enough, his voice came over her answering
machine once it picked up.

"Jessie, if you're there pick up." He was using his
drill sergeant voice again. "We need to talk. Pick
up."

She drowned him out by turning the Genesis song
playing on her compact alarm clock/radio up full
blast. The music filled her bedroom as she returned
to her walk-in closet and tossed an unwanted pair of
aqua sweatpants over her shoulder. What had she
been thinking when she bought them? She never wore
aqua. Out. They were going out. And so were her
worries about Curt.

He had no power here. She was in her own domain.
Mistress of all she surveyed. Sitting on the carpeted
floor, with a pile of clothes beside her, she paused to
view the rest of the room.

Her bedroom, and indeed the entire condo, was
done in a relaxed cottage style. The white four-poster

bed was covered with a pastel duvet cover in shades of rose and cream. The mellow pine dresser had been a find at the Kane County Flea Market, as was the chair beside it on which she'd painted a whimsical cherub motif. In the far corner was her favorite curl-up-and-read chair, casually slipcovered in pink-and-cream ticking material. The walls were painted a soft sage-green the exact color of the ceramic bowl on top of the dresser. She could still remember the day her mom had bought it for her from an artisan at Chicago's Gold Coast Art Show as a college graduation present.

She'd never told her mom about Curt, about her feelings for him back in high school or that night. Her mom had been busy trying to keep the bill collectors at bay. She didn't need any more problems. After many years of working full-time, her mom had recently retired and was now fulfilling a lifelong dream of taking a month-long cruise in the South Pacific with a good friend of hers.

Jessica couldn't imagine being away from her home for a month. This was her center, her base, surrounded by the things she loved.

But not by the man you loved.

When Jessica was eighteen, this wasn't the way she'd pictured her life. She'd thought she'd have a family of her own by now. A boy and a girl. Maybe even two boys and two girls. She'd be a stay-at-home mom until the youngest one was in first grade. And on their birthday she'd make them a cake from scratch and throw them the best party a child ever had.

Not like her own childhood birthdays, which always seemed to fall shortly after a new move. As the brand-new kid on the block, there were no friends to invite to her party. So no one had come, including her own father. Her mother tried to make up for it, however there was only so much one woman could do.

No, that big family Jessica had envisioned had not come to pass. She had no children of her own. No family of her own. Here she was, almost thirty and still alone.

You have options, she reminded herself. *There are plenty of kids waiting to be adopted. It's time you stopped waiting for something that wasn't going to happen and did something to help someone else.*

Somewhere there was a child that needed her, a child waiting for her love.

This wasn't a new idea. It had been percolating in the back of her mind for a year or more. She'd even gone so far as getting the phone number of various state and private adoption agencies. But she hadn't made any calls. Until today.

Perched on the edge of her bed, her feet curled beneath her, she called the two largest agencies and asked them to send her information about single-parent adoptions.

Hanging up the phone, she felt better. Felt more in charge of her own destiny. Now she just wished that she'd kept her mouth shut and not let her anger get the best of her with Curt.

She hated that she'd let him know that she couldn't have children. She didn't want his pity, didn't want anything from him.

Which got her to thinking, how well did she really

know Curt? Even back then, when they'd been teenagers, how well had she really known him?

Yes, they'd gotten as physically intimate as two
people could be. Sure she'd shared one life-altering
evening in the back seat of his Mustang, giving him
her virginity. Not that it had been much of a gift. Bad
boys like Curt hadn't been in the market for nerdy
inexperienced girls like her. They'd wanted popular
cheerleaders with big busts and long legs.

But she'd loved him from afar for so long—from
her freshman year on. Tutoring him their senior year
had provided the proximity for that crush to grow into
monumental proportions. And when she'd run into
him behind the library the night of their senior prom,
she'd thought it was fate. While the girls in her class
had been decked out in expensive trendy gowns with
floral corsages, dancing the night away, she'd spent
that time with Curt.

He was right about one thing. He had had too much
to drink that night. That's why she'd offered to drive
him home. He'd told her he didn't have a home, and
told her to drive out to one of the forest preserves that
ringed the city.

She'd known what she was doing even if he hadn't.
Not that she'd thought things through, like birth control. If she'd planned that far ahead, it was to assume
he'd have something with him. He hadn't. She'd
hadn't cared.

They'd both been foolish. Scratch that, they'd both
been downright *stupid*. Dangerously so. It wasn't as
if she believed that rumor that you couldn't get pregnant your first time. She hadn't cared. She'd been that
blind.

As for Curt, well he hadn't seemed to be able to get enough of her. Kissing her with thrusts of his tongue that had at first scared her a bit and then tempted her to give him more. And she had. Gladly. Willingly. Passionately.

But how well did she really know him? Even now?

She knew he joined the Marines because he wanted to see the world, but she also knew that there was more he wasn't telling her even about that one thing in his life. She knew he had a daughter, but she didn't know the circumstances that had led to her birth. She knew he was a man who valued honor, but she didn't know if he honored her.

The series of Genesis songs on the radio finished, allowing her to hear the doorbell pealing. Jeez, the pizza! She'd almost forgotten she'd ordered it.

"Coming," she cried out, grabbing her wallet from her purse as she passed by the pine table in her foyer on her way to the front door. She was dressed in gray drawstring knit pants and a well-worn Taste Of Chicago T-shirt, not that the pizza deliveryman would care. "Sorry about that..."

But it wasn't the pizza man. It was the U.S. Marine man. Curt. Still wearing his dress blues.

She hadn't considered this option, him just showing up at her front door. "What are you doing here? How did you even know where I live?" she demanded. "And where's Blue?"

"She's with a sitter, and I knew where you lived because I followed you home from Dino's after we ate there the other day."

"You were stalking me?" Her voice reflected her outrage.

"Negative." His voice revealed his leashed irritation. "I was making sure you got home okay. Why didn't you answer the phone?"

"I thought that would be obvious." Jessica tightened her hold on the door. "Because I didn't want to speak to you."

"You think you can just dump something on me the way you did and walk out?"

"Affirmative," she retorted, tossing one of his own phrases back at him.

"Well, you're mistaken," he said curtly.

"No, *you're* the one who is mistaken. This is my home, and you're not welcome here."

Mrs. Leibowitz, her neighbor across the hall, opened her door while keeping the chain on. Peering out suspiciously, she said, "Are you okay, Jessica? Why is there a Marine at your door? Is there something wrong?" Her voice was raised in alarm. "Are we under attack or something?"

"No, Mrs. Leibowitz," Jessica hurriedly assured her. "There's nothing to worry about." Aware of her neighbor's well-meaning curiosity, as well as Curt's well-known stubbornness, Jessica decided to confront Curt in the privacy of her own home rather than out in the hallway. Opening the door wider for him to come in, she spoke softly as he passed her, so that only he could hear her. "You've got five minutes."

He made the most use of his time by getting right to the point. "Why didn't you tell me right from the start that we'd made love all those years ago?"

"Because you didn't even recognize me at first," she replied. "And once you did, you showed no signs of acknowledging anything that occurred between us."

"Because I—"

"Didn't remember." She interrupted him. "I really don't need to hear yet again how forgettable I am."

"It wasn't you. It was me. I had a hazy memory of us in the car, but the next day had I such a hangover that I didn't trust those memories. I didn't think they could possibly be accurate. You, Jessie the Brain, with me? How likely was that? What was I supposed to say to you? Hey, I've got these hot fantasies, and I'm not sure if they're real or not. How far did we go in the back seat of my car? I'm sure that would have gone over real well."

"Why do you even care?"

"Because I care about you."

"Yeah, right," she scoffed.

"I want you to tell me exactly what happened that night," he ordered.

"Forget it." Her voice was just as tough as his.

He relented. "All right, just give me an overview," he said. "We made love in the back seat of my car?" She nodded. "You were a virgin?" She nodded. "Did I..." He paused to swallow. "Did I...force you? Coerce you in any way? Is that why you're so angry with me?"

This time she shook her head. "No," she said quietly. "You didn't force me. I knew what I was doing. I knew it wasn't right, but I couldn't seem to help myself."

"And we...um...we didn't use any protection?"

She shook her head again. "I thought you'd have

something, but you didn't. And I wasn't exactly planning on doing anything like that that night."

"Then why did you?"

She wasn't about to tell him how much she'd loved him back then, as only an eighteen-year-old can. "I...I got caught up in the passion of the moment."

"And afterward, you thought you were pregnant?"

She turned away from him. "I told you that already."

He reached out for her arm, halting her in her tracks. "Then tell me something else. What did you mean when you said that there never would be a baby, not for you?"

She wrapped her arms around her middle, loosening his hold on her. "I don't want to talk about it."

"Did something happen?" he pressed her. "Something that prevented you from having kids?"

"Something you did, you mean? Something for you to feel guilty about?"

"I already feel guilty," he quietly said.

"Then don't. You weren't at fault. No one was. You don't want to hear all the medical details and trust me, I don't want to tell them to you. The bottom line is that I can't have kids. These things just happen sometimes."

It didn't matter what she said. For Curt, it was history repeating itself. Him—screwing up. He felt as if he were fifteen again, a notorious troublemaker who'd been warned he'd come to no good. He'd had sex with Jessie while he was drunk. And despite what she said about him not coercing her, he doubted that "doing the deed" had been her idea. No, he'd been the one who had set things into motion, and then walked off. What if she had gotten pregnant?

The fact that he didn't remember the details was no excuse in his book. He'd known they'd made out, even if he hadn't known how far it had gone. When he'd returned from boot camp, he'd avoided her. She was right about that. He hadn't wanted to deal with what might have happened. So he'd shoved it, and her, aside.

So much for being honorable.

But that was twelve years ago. He had a second chance now to do the right thing. He could marry her.

He'd been considering the idea for a while now. Thinking he had nothing to offer her, he had dismissed the idea. But now that he knew about her inability to have children of her own, he realized that he did have something. Or *someone*. Blue.

He knew how much Jessie loved Blue. He could see it every time the two of them were together.

It would be the perfect solution. For both him and Jessie. It wasn't as if she found him physically repulsive. Quite the opposite. The attraction was still between them. That kiss they'd shared had been hot. And he'd caught her looking at him a time or two, the way a woman looks when she's interested.

It was time to set things in motion. So he said the words.

"Marry me."

She stared at him as if he'd lost his mind. Maybe he should have worked his way into it, instead of just bluntly stating it like that. Women liked flowery words. Not that he was any good at that stuff.

"Are you crazy?" she said.

Not exactly the response Curt was looking for. But he refused to be discouraged. "No, I'm not crazy."

"Then why do you want to marry me?"

Danger—land mines. The warning flashed in his head as he tried to maneuver his way safely through an answer that wouldn't trigger her anger. "Why shouldn't I want to marry you?"

Not the most brilliant of replies. All it did was buy him some time. And she looked like she knew it, too.

"You're an attractive, smart, sexy woman," he quickly added. "We share a past. We also share some pretty powerful chemistry. Or are you going to deny that?"

He was hoping she would, that way he could kiss her and prove his point. In his scenario, she'd melt in his arms and accept his proposal. Hey, it could happen.

She stepped into his trap, just not the way he thought she would.

"Chemistry?" she repeated. "We've only kissed once..."

"I can remedy that," Curt murmured.

He claimed her mouth with a gentleness intended to reassure her that they were meant to be together, that she had no reason to fear him. Keeping his passion at bay, he slowly deepened the pressure of his lips on hers, inviting her participation but not demanding it.

Having expected a more forceful approach, she was both startled and disarmed by this tenderness. Unspoken was the vow that the kiss would deepen only as she permitted. The thought of her having even that much power over him was a heady thing. She controlled the tempo of the kiss.

Her eyelids fluttered shut as she let his mouth do the rest of the convincing. His tongue traced the outline of her lips, coaxing and promising instead of conquering. But in the end, she was unable to resist the intoxicating potency of his kiss. Sliding her arms up around his neck, she parted her lips and allowed him to taste her response.

When she did so, his mouth engulfed hers in a turbulent seeking of souls. Her body was on fire as he drew her ever closer, gliding his hands beneath her T-shirt with sensual stealth. He undid the front fastening of her bra and then cupped her breast in the palm of his hand, stroking her nipple with his thumb.

Her startled gasp of pleasure was incorporated into their next kiss as his tongue met hers with impassioned need. Their embrace became increasingly intimate, the brass buttons of his uniform pressed against her freed breasts as his hand slipped around her waist to the small of her back. His fingers pressed against her bare skin, making her shiver and burn at the same time.

Gradually the ringing in her ears increased. It wasn't until it was accompanied by the sound of someone shouting "Pizza Delivery!" outside her front door that she realized what was going on.

Tearing herself from Curt's embrace, she put her trembling fingers to her lips. What had she been thinking?

"I'll be there in a second," she shouted to the deliveryman even as she turned her back on Curt and refastened her bra. It took her two attempts, but she got it done. She also grabbed the money she'd left on the foyer pine table as she opened the door.

"One medium Hawaiian pizza with extra ham and pineapple," the teenager said, handing over the pizza after removing it from its thermal wrapping.

She paid for it, including a generous tip, even as Curt was saying, "Pineapple and ham? On a pizza?"

"It's my house, I can eat whatever I want," she growled, leaving him in the hallway as she headed for her kitchen where she slapped the pizza on the white-tiled table.

"Sure you can eat whatever you want," Curt said as he followed her. He was using that voice men used when they thought they were dealing with an irrational woman.

Despite that heated embrace they'd just shared, she wasn't fooled. Yes, Curt wanted her. Yes, there was definitely a powerful attraction between them. But it wasn't as if he was suddenly in love with her.

No, he'd proposed to her so that he would have someone to take care of his daughter.

Okay, so maybe he wanted her as his wife because he was feeling a little guilty about what had happened that night when they made love. But the main reason was because of Blue.

She shouldn't blame him for loving his daughter. She shouldn't feel such pain because he didn't love her. What she should do was turn him down. "I'm not marrying you," she told him.

"Why not?"

Because you don't love me. Because you don't feel the same way I do. Because I deserve more than just sex. Because I'm not sure you even know what love is yet, or that you ever will.

"Because I don't want to," she replied.

"Are you saying you don't want me?"

Denying that would be pointless. And it would just give him an excuse to kiss her again. So instead she said, "No, I'm just saying I don't want to marry you."

"Why not?" he repeated.

She shot him an irritable look. "Listen, this isn't an essay question here. A proposal requires a simple yes or no answer. And I said no."

"Now you're sounding like a teacher."

"I *am* a teacher."

"And I don't hold that against you."

"How generous of you."

Curt heard the anger in her voice. He wasn't just generous, he could be patient, too. When the situation warranted it. Because he was determined that he'd win in the end.

She hadn't said no because of his limp. She didn't find him physically unappealing, which was a huge relief. He knew a beat-up Marine like him was no matrimonial prize, but he also knew he and Jessie would be good together. More than good. Incredible.

But he needed more to go on here. He needed to know what was going on inside of Jessie's head—never an easy matter for him where women were concerned.

Jessie wanted him, he knew she did. That kiss had just given him a heart attack, leaving his body painfully aching, and not because of his bum leg. She'd made him forget his own name, made him so hungry for her that he'd wanted to lower her to the floor, peel all her clothes off and take her right there and then. But he hadn't. Surely that proved he cared about her? That he cared about her feelings?

So why didn't she want to marry him? It would be the perfect solution. To both their problems. She'd get the family she seemed to want so badly. And he'd get someone to help take care of Blue.

It was a perfect plan. Jessie just needed some time to get used to the idea. Or he had to get her used to the idea, make it seem so appealing that she couldn't continue turning him down.

"I know why you're doing this," she stated. Her defensive posture warned him that she was in no mood for convincing at this time.

"And why is that?"

"You didn't propose to me because you love me, because you've suddenly gotten all romantic about our future together. No, you did it for the simple reason that you want someone to take care of Blue for you."

There was nothing simple about his feelings for Jessie. And she clearly didn't appreciate being proposed to because of Blue. Curt could understand that. Jessie wanted to be needed for herself. She needed to be…courted.

The old-fashioned word came to him in a flash. That's how he could win her over. By courting her.

Not that he had a clue how to do that. His relationships with women in the past had been fairly direct, with both parties in search of a good time without any strings. But he'd find out everything there was to know about courting. It would be his mission, one he'd undertake with the dedication and determination of a career Marine. He could do this. He *would* do this.

"I think you should leave now," Jessica was saying as she headed for the front door, which she held open in a clear indication of her eagerness to get rid of him.

"All right, I'll go." He needed time to research courting stuff. He was certainly no pro in that department, but his buddy Joe Wilder was. "I'll be back."

"Don't bother."

"It's no bother, ma'am," he drawled, gently running his index finger down her cheek to the corner of her mouth. "It'll be a pleasure convincing you."

"That won't happen," she declared.

Curt smiled confidently. "We'll see."

She slammed the door in his face.

Turning to find Mrs. Leibowitz peering out at him through a crack in her door across the hallway, he cheerfully told her, "This Marine is going to marry your neighbor. How would you like to come to the wedding, ma'am?"

Gasping her outrage, Mrs. Leibowitz slammed her door shut.

Chapter Nine

"Improvise, overcome and adapt. Those are my mottos," Curt told his buddy Joe when he finally reached him on the phone a few days later. He'd called Joe for advice. Instead his friend was giving him grief.

"Are you working up a battle plan or courting a woman?" Joe countered in a mocking drawl.

"What's the difference?" Curt replied.

"Jeez, Blackwell, you're worse off than I thought. You proposed to this Jessica and she did not react well, huh?"

"I never had to chase after a woman before," Curt said. "What are you laughing at?"

"Your ability to put your foot in your mouth. So you called me because, lacking your charming nature, I *have* had to chase after the women in my life, right? You're just lucky I'm not a sensitive guy or I'd be insulted."

"You're not in special training at Marine Corps Combat Development Command Quantico because you're a sensitive guy," Curt retorted. "You're smart, you know how to get people to do what you want."

"So do you."

"She's a civilian. I can't *order* her to marry me. Well, I can, but she doesn't respond well to orders."

"Surprise, surprise," Joe drawled. "No wonder your mission was not successful."

Curt gritted his teeth. "You've never had to work hard to get a woman to like you, although I have no idea why you're so popular with the female population."

"Hey, that works two ways. I have no idea why women flock after you, unless it's something to do with the dark and brooding mysterious loner thing you've got going. But apparently that act doesn't work on this woman."

"You've got that right," Curt muttered.

"Then what does work?"

Curt bluntly replied, "Kissing her."

"That's it?"

"And having her spend time with Blue."

"Then go with those two things," Joe said. "Throw in some flowers, some romantic words and bingo, you're home free. Although why you'd want to enter into the institution of marriage is beyond me. I know, I know, you told me it was for your kid. But I'm still having a hard time picturing you as a husband."

Curt wasn't about to admit he was having the same problem himself.

"Just keep this in mind, Blackwell. Romance is a

battlefield filled with land mines, and you've got to
tread carefully or get blown to bits. That's my Wild-
erism for the day.''

"I already figured that much out for myself," Curt
retorted.

"Then you're ahead of the game. Good luck,
buddy." Joe laughed before adding, "I have a feeling
you're gonna need it."

In the end Curt decided to go with what he knew,
Marine battle tactics. Infiltrate the enemy camp and
gain pertinent information. Search for a weakness and
utilize it.

So the first thing he did the next morning was talk
to Jessica's co-workers, interrogating them one at a
time.

He spoke to the youngest one first. Lisa was her
name. He was there early and Blue had gone to speak
to Jessica, allowing him to speak to Lisa privately for
a moment or two. He didn't have time for small talk,
the rest of the kids would be barging in any minute.

He got right to the point. "Tell me what Jessie's
favorite things are. What does she like?"

"Marines in dress blues," Lisa replied with a saucy
grin. "And she's not alone in that." The meaning in
her brown eyes was clear, sending out blatant *I'm
available* signals.

This pretty young thing was giving him the green
light, and he felt nothing. He hadn't had to court her,
hadn't had to do anything. He wasn't even wearing
dress blues, just his regulation camouflage. Even so
she was letting him know she was interested. But he
didn't feel anything. He wasn't the least bit tempted.

He would have worried that the sniper's bullet had left him with more than a bum leg were it not for the fact that he just about went off like a firecracker whenever Jessie was around.

If he was only looking to marry someone just to watch Blue, Lisa would be good. But telling Jessie that wouldn't do him any good. Telling her that he wanted her in his bed wouldn't do the trick, either. No, he had to get this courting thing mastered.

"Ma'am, I just want to know about Jessie," Curt steadfastly maintained.

"Well..." Lisa bit her lip as she thought a moment. "She's loyal and true, like the U.S. Marines. Her favorite ice cream is Chunky Monkey, she's allergic to shellfish, has a weakness for barbecued potato chips, and is a big Genesis fan. That help?"

"It's a start. Thank you, ma'am."

"You could ask her this yourself, you know," Lisa said.

"Negative, ma'am. And don't tell her I asked you about her, okay?"

Leaning closer, Lisa whispered, "So this is a covert operation, hmm?"

Curt nodded. "Affirmative, ma'am."

"My lips are sealed. Are you going to speak to Tawanna, too?"

"Later," he replied, noting the suspicious and disapproving looks Jessie was shooting his way. But before he could make his getaway, Tawanna approached him on her own.

"I sure hope you're not going to turn into pond scum," the older African-American woman said, her dark eyes flashing.

"Pardon me, ma'am?"

Propping her hands on her ample hips, Tawanna said, "I saw Lisa flirting with you."

"Then you should also have seen that I wasn't flirting back."

"I just wanted to be real sure about that."

"Be sure. I'm interested in Jessie. And I could use your help, ma'am." He had a feeling that throwing himself on the older woman's mercy would work well, and it did.

She thawed considerably. "About time you asked me. But we can't talk here. I'll give you my phone number, and you can call me." Reaching into the pocket of her colorful jumper, she pulled out a piece of paper and pen. Scribbling the information down, she handed it to him.

Jessica couldn't believe what she was seeing. First Curt hits on Lisa, and now Tawanna. Did the man have no conscience? What was he doing? she wondered bitterly. Asking them to marry him now that she'd said no? Was she so easily replaceable? Preschool teacher, preschool teaching assistants, it didn't matter. Nineteen years old or fifty, that made no difference. Curt just wanted a wife.

Okay, so she was probably overreacting here. She should just ask Lisa and Tawanna what they were talking about with Curt.

"I don't remember," Lisa replied, despite the fact that Curt had only left less than five minutes ago. "It wasn't anything important." But her gaze slid away from Jessica's face as if she were hiding something.

Tawanna was equally evasive. "What did we discuss? Nothing much. We didn't talk for more than a second or two.''

"I saw you give him a piece of paper.''

Tawanna shrugged. "A book I was recommending.''

"Is that right? Which one?''

"Why the interrogation, girlfriend?'' Tawanna gave her a direct look as she asked, "Something going on I should know about?''

"No.'' Jessica wasn't about to confess that Curt had proposed to her last night. Her feelings were still too raw, too contradictory. Part of her wanted to believe that he did want her and no one else. Part of her wanted to run in the other direction before she got hurt.

Do you really think he could love you? a tiny voice in her head mocked her. *Why should he? Your own father couldn't love you. Face it, you're just not the kind of woman that men fall head over heels for.*

"Jessie, you look sad,'' Blue noted, tugging on Jessie's hand to get her attention. "Blue's sad, too.''

Jessie knelt down beside her. "Why are you sad, Blue?''

"'Cause I was bad and kicked those girls in ballet. Kicking is bad.''

"Kicking *is* bad,'' Jessie agreed. "You might have hurt those girls.''

"Blue is bad.''

"Blue did a bad thing, but she's not bad. *Kicking* is bad.''

"Is Daddy going to give me back?'' Blue whispered.

"Oh, honey.'' Blinking away her own tears, Jessie

engulfed Blue in a big hug. "No way, sweetie. Your Daddy loves you very much."

"Mommy left me when she went dead. Don't want Daddy to leave me."

"He won't leave you." As a result of his leg injury, Curt had been relegated to a desk job, which she knew didn't please him any. But at least he was safe. And even if he was transferred elsewhere, he'd bring Blue as well. Although the thought of the little girl having to move around the way Jessica had as a child brought a pang to her heart.

"Will *you* leave me?" Blue asked, her brown eyes so like Curt's as they gravely stared at her.

Jessica knew the little girl was looking for reassurance, that the attachment Blue felt for her was only that of a child who'd recently lost her mother, that Blue would grow and move on. The years would pass and maybe, if Jessica was lucky, Blue would retain fond memories of the preschool teacher who'd been nice to her.

Logically Jessica knew all that, yet it didn't seem to stop her heart from melting, didn't stop her from loving Blue.

But loving Blue didn't mean that marrying her father, who didn't love Jessica and might never do so, was a good idea.

"I'll always be your friend and if you ever need me, I'll help you," Jessica promised. "There will always be someone to take care of you. When your daddy is working, then Lisa, Tawanna and I take care of you."

"You and my daddy both take care of me."

Jessica nodded. "That's right."

"Okay." Smiling now and clearly satisfied with Jessica's response, Blue quickly moved on to something else, heading for her friend Susan to help her work a puzzle.

Watching her, Jessica wished it were that easy to quiet her own fears, that she could get over her own emotional issues with the trusting confidence of a three-year-old.

Blue may have moved on, but she hadn't forgotten. Later that day, Blue used her time in the art corner to make a drawing with three figures. "My family," she proudly told Jessica. "Daddy, me and you."

This time the pain caught Jessica by surprise. So did the intensity with which she wanted what was in that childish drawing—a family, a family that loved her.

As soon as he got Blue to bed that night, Curt called in reinforcements. He called Tawanna.

"Took you long enough," the older woman scoffed.

"Well, ma'am," he began, "I don't know how much Jessie has told you—"

"Nothing," she interrupted him to say. "But even if she had, I won't go breaking any confidences." Her voice carried a clear warning.

"And I wouldn't ask you to," he quickly assured her. "I'm just looking for some advice here, ma'am."

"That shows good sense on your part."

"Thank you, ma'am."

"Don't go ma'aming me," she scolded him. "Makes me feel older than I am, and I'm old enough as it is. Call me Tawanna."

To him any woman he didn't know was a ma'am, regardless of her age. And any man he didn't know was a sir. It was all part of a Marine's discipline.

Semper Gumby. Be flexible.

"Okay, Tawanna. I'll try to remember that," he said.

"You do that. And remember that a little romance never hurt. I went with a soldier once. In the Army."

Curt winced but didn't correct her by saying a U.S. Marine was not a soldier. He was a Marine, always with a capital *M*.

"He was always so…practical." Tawanna made the word sound like an insult. "No soul, y'know?"

"Not really."

"You need to let Jessica know how important she is to you. As important as, say, the U.S. Marines. Think you can do that?"

Curt supposed this would fall under the *adapt* portion of his improvise, overcome and adapt battle plan. Not that Jessie wasn't important to him, because she was. But nothing had ever played as big a role in his life as the United States Marine Corps. He'd been a Marine for twelve years. He'd only been a dad for a month. And he'd only been a wanna-be husband for a week. But if he wanted to accomplish his mission, then he had to act on the information provided to him.

"I can do that," he declared without any sign of doubt.

The next night, Curt called Jessica, all in a dither. That alone warned her that something was up, because despite his inexperience, he never sounded this flustered. Not even when she'd gone to his apartment

for Daddy Boot Camp and he had jam on his face.
No doubt it was against United States Marine Corps
policy to get flustered.

And the reason for his extreme agitation? He'd decided he couldn't face life without her? He wanted to
declare his undying love for her?

No. Of course not.

He'd called because Blue had somehow, he wasn't
real clear of the details, gotten a wad of chewing gum
stuck in her hair.

"Can you come over and help me?" he asked,
sounding so forlorn she almost automatically said yes.

"There's no need for that. I can tell you over the
phone what to do."

"Everything I did just made it worse. I'm not good
with hair," Curt said.

While it was true that he was no Vidal Sassoon,
Blue's pigtails, when she wore them, were no longer
completely lopsided. Occasionally the little girl even
had a few daisy or Disney character hair clips that
had been placed in her hair with a military precision
that only Curt could have provided.

So what was really going on here? Could Curt really sink so low as to use his daughter to get to her?
Or was Jessica being overly suspicious? What if Blue
really did need her help? What if Curt really did chop
her hair badly in his efforts to get the gum out? What
if the other kids then ridiculed Blue because of her
strangely hacked haircut? It would all be Jessica's
fault.

"If this is a hoax just to get me over to your place,
you're going to be *very* sorry," she warned him.

"Will you come over?"

"All right. But I'm not staying."

She considered changing her clothes. The Save The Children sweatshirt was comfortable, as were the black leggings she wore with it, but they weren't real flattering.

What did she care? As if it mattered what she wore. She was only going to Curt's apartment for Blue's sake. And the little one didn't care what Jessica wore. For that matter, she doubted that Curt cared what she wore, either.

Jessica was at Curt's front door within fifteen minutes. He led her straight into Blue's bedroom, where the little girl was sitting on her bed waiting for her.

When Jessica saw the matted gum in Blue's hair, she felt badly for suspecting Curt of luring her here under false pretenses. "I'll need scissors and an ice cube," she told Curt. Turning to Blue, she said, "We'll have you fixed up in no time, honey."

After getting the items she requested, Curt said, "I'll just leave you two alone," and beat a hasty retreat. Or attempted to.

Jessica didn't let him get very far. "Hold it. You're not going anywhere," she firmly informed him. "You're going to have to learn how to manage this by yourself next time. So watch and learn. Here, sit on the other side of Blue and hold the rest of her hair out of the way."

For a man who didn't like obeying orders from civilians, he obeyed hers quickly enough. It didn't take Jessica long to realize that this might not have been the wisest move on her part. Curt was close enough for her to feel the warmth of his breath on her cheek as she bent closer to apply the ice cube to the wad of gum.

Suddenly she was all thumbs. The slippery ice cube slid from her fingers and flew over Blue's head to land in...Curt's lap.

Which wouldn't have been so bad had he been wearing jeans instead of a thin pair of khaki slacks. To give him credit, he didn't yelp and leap to his feet. Instead he gave her a wry look that lingered, the heated intensity in his brown eyes warming her heart...and the rest of her body as well. Aware that her cheeks were flushed, she tried not to let him see how flustered she was.

An impossible task. She might as well have tried to build the Great Wall of China between them. No can do.

"I believe this is yours, ma'am," he drawled, taking her hand and placing the now rapidly melting ice cube in her palm. The contrast of the cold ice and his warm fingertips brushing against her skin was incredibly sensual.

Excitement surged through her veins like a fine wine. "I...uh..." She had to unglue her tongue from the roof of her mouth before being able to speak coherently. "I think I'll try a new ice cube."

She dropped the one he'd handed her back into the bowl and picked up a new one, tempted to run its coolness over her hot cheeks. She had to get a grip here. She was acting like an idiot. She was acting like Jessie the Brain, social misfit from her high school days, who stumbled over her words and never seemed able to say the right thing around other people.

Okay, she refused to give in to this. Concentrating

on what she was doing, she carefully applied the ice. "You do this until the gum freezes and then carefully peel the gum off the hair."

For her part, Blue was remarkably patient for a three-year-old, not wiggling or complaining. She appeared happy just to have her father and Jessica by her side. She became most unhappy when Jessica appeared to be leaving. Blue's tears started immediately and didn't dry until Jessica promised to help Blue with her bath, which then became a bath and a hair wash. Then there was her bedtime story, which both Jessica and Curt had to read to her.

Jessica was touched by the way Curt read *Goodnight Moon*. He had such an expressive voice it was a shame he didn't use his non-Marine voice more often. Looking around the room, she had to admit that he hadn't spared any expense in making his daughter a special place to call home. But it took more than furniture and books—it took love.

And while Curt clearly cared for his daughter, there was still a certain distance in his approach to her, as if he continued to be unsure of his role in her life. He didn't seem able to simply open his heart and lavish Blue with love the way Jessica longed to. But he was making progress, considering how distant he'd been that first day in her classroom.

Blue insisted Jessica stay a little longer, despite the fact that the little girl's eyelids were fluttering with exhaustion. Jessica sang her a lullaby her mother used to sing to her when she was little and they'd moved to a new place. Jessica hummed the bits she didn't know and Blue was asleep by the second verse.

Moving cautiously, Jessica removed her hand from

Blue's. She tucked the blanket up over the little girl's shoulders. Leaning down to brush her lips against Blue's baby-soft cheek, Jessica gave herself the luxury of whispering, "I love you, sweetie."

Then she forced herself to step away. This wasn't her little girl, wasn't her family, wasn't her life. Gathering her composure, Jessica walked into the living room. "She's asleep now—" Her words stopped as she realized that Curt had dimmed the lights and lit the place with several candles. A Genesis song was softly playing in the background.

"What do you think you're doing?" she demanded.

"Trying to seduce you," he instantly replied. "Am I having any luck yet?"

She had to laugh at his blunt candor, not to mention the hopeful look in his eyes. This was a new Curt, one she hadn't seen before but one she'd glimpsed in Blue's bedroom earlier. This was a Curt she wasn't sure how to resist. Defying the authoritative Marine barking orders had been a piece of cake. But this man had a track record of working his magic on her.

"No luck yet?" His inflection reflected his humor. "Then how about this?" He handed her a large gift bag.

"What's this?"

"Look inside and find out."

She did and couldn't believe what she found. A bag of barbecued potato chips. It was even the brand she liked. But there was more. A Genesis Greatest Hits CD. A bottle of her favorite perfumed shower gel. And a plush toy dragon with a cheerful grin. She ran a trembling finger over that grin.

Curt broke the silence, his voice uncharacteristically soft. "Remember in high school at the Halloween carnival how much you wanted to win a dragon? I got detention and had to work the booth, a creative punishment from that long-haired English teacher... what was his name again?"

"Mr. Ivanhoe," she replied in a slightly unsteady voice. "But he liked us to call him Phil."

"That's right. Anyway I remember you really wanting that dragon and not getting it."

She remembered it, too. The dragon at the carnival had been the twin of one she'd seen in a store when she was about eight. Even after all these years she could still hear her father's voice. *If you get straight A's in school, I'll get you that dragon.*

She'd run home with her report card and impatiently waited in the driveway for him to come home. It had been dark and supper was long over, but she'd still waited. *Look, Daddy, I got all A's!*

He'd ignored her.

My dragon, Daddy. You promised.

She no longer remembered the exact wording of his excuses—the bottom line was that it was time to move on to another job, and he hadn't gotten the dragon for her.

Stop your pouting. It was just a stupid dragon. If you behave I promise to come to that birthday party of yours in a few weeks.

He hadn't done that, either.

It was the last time she'd trusted any of her father's promises, but not the last time she'd wished that those promises had been kept.

So yes, when she'd seen a similar dragon at the

Halloween carnival in high school, she'd gone after it, hoping to recapture those lost promises. Because in some way that dragon had represented her chance at happiness, and she'd been determined to get it for herself instead of being disappointed by others. But it hadn't been meant to be. Again, the dragon had gotten away.

Until now. She ran her finger over the dragon's grin once more, as if unable to comprehend that she finally held it in her own two hands. "I can't believe you did this."

"Do you like it?"

She nodded, the emotion so great that she couldn't find words to express it. "More than I can say."

"There's also Chunky Monkey ice cream in the freezer. Want some?"

She swallowed the lump in her throat as she shook her head. "Not now, thanks."

"Did I get it right? Your favorite things, I mean."

"Yes, you did." She stared at the table filled with an array of goodies that were more dear to her than gold, because he'd taken the time to get them for her, because he'd remembered an incident she'd long forgotten but had yet to overcome. "I don't know what to say."

"Say you'll go out with me Friday night. Just the two of us. I'll get a sitter for Blue. Come on," he coaxed her, with his bad boy smile, the one he saved for special occasions, the one that never failed to get to her. "Say yes."

She stared down at the dragon, wondering if once again it represented her chance at happiness. Here she was, after all these years, with both the dragon and

Curt within reach. Maybe it was a sign? Maybe it meant she'd have a chance at happiness after all. All she had to do was grab hold with both hands. To take that chance. "Yes," she said,

"You won't regret it," Curt promised her,

Jessica sincerely hoped not, because she didn't know if she could take any more broken promises.

Chapter Ten

"I leave town for a weekend and come back to find you've dumped Trevor and are dating Curt Bad Boy Blackwell. I don't believe this!" Amy had her leg slung over the arm of Jessica's favorite curl-up-and-read chair in her bedroom.

"Stop complaining and help me find something to wear," Jessica demanded from inside the walk-in closet.

"You're even starting to sound like him," Amy grumbled as she took a bite of an apple.

Jessica popped out of the closet to ask, "Which of these two do you like better? This one..." Jessica held up an ivory print georgette dress. "Or this one?" She swapped hangers to hold up the blue silk dress she'd worn the last time she'd gone out with Trevor.

"The first one makes you look like a schoolteacher and you end up wearing the second one whenever you go out."

"You're not being helpful here. What am I going to wear?"

"Where is he taking you?" Amy asked.

"Out to dinner."

"Where? At Dino's?"

"I didn't ask him."

"First mistake," Amy muttered before taking another bite of apple.

"I thought you said my first mistake was saying yes."

"And having made that mistake you compounded matters by not clarifying where you were going."

Eyeing the blue dress, which it was true she seemed to have worn a lot, Jessica noted, "I think he said he was taking me someplace nice."

"You *think* he said?"

"I was still stunned by all those wonderful things he got me." She motioned to the items on display atop her pine dresser. "A dragon, Amy. He got me a dragon."

"So you've told me for the past three hours."

"It hasn't been that long..." Jessica paused to check her watch. "Oh, no, he'll be here in two hours! And I haven't done my hair yet!"

"Don't panic," Amy told her, leaping from the chair to march into Jessica's closet herself. A minute later she was back. "I think you should wear this."

The black sleeveless sheath dress still had the price tag on it. Jessica hadn't worn it because it was shorter than any of her other dresses and frankly she'd always chickened out.

"You don't think it's too..." Jessica wiggled her hand.

"Of course it's *too*," Amy mocked her. "That's why you should wear it tonight. It's chic and elegant. Very Audrey Hepburn. And yes, it's shorter than what you usually wear, but I thought you wanted Curt to notice you, right?"

"Right."

"Then wear this. And forget about those sensible black pumps of yours. Dig out those darling little three-inch spike heels with the ankle strap that you wore to my office party last Christmas."

"You made me buy those." Jessica's voice was accusatory.

Amy was not the least bit repentant. "Good thing, too, because they'll look like dynamite with this dress. Okay, now that we've made those fashion decisions, tell me again why you dumped Trevor in favor of Curt."

"I did not dump Trevor," Jessica denied. "We mutually decided we weren't suited and that was weeks ago now. And I'm not dating Curt, we're just going out on a date. One date. The only date I've ever had with Curt."

"So you're considering this to be like the senior prom you missed out on, huh?"

"No. He got me a dragon, Amy. He remembered how much I wanted it. I swear to you, I never said a word to him. How could I? I'd practically forgotten all about it."

"The same way you'd *practically* forgotten about Curt before he walked into your classroom?" Amy countered astutely.

Now it was Jessica's turn to sink into the slipcovered chair to gaze at her friend with earnest solemnity.

"What if I was wrong in thinking that he only asked me to marry him because of Blue. What if he's starting to feel for me the way I feel for him?"

"Which is?"

"That he's the one. That he was always the one. I think you were right. The real reason I couldn't accept Jeff's proposal last year was because I never really got over Curt."

"I said that?"

"You did. At Dino's when we ate cheeseburgers after Curt kissed me the first time."

"The *first* time? So he's kissed you more than once?"

"He kissed me after he proposed to me and I said no."

"No doubt in the hopes of convincing you to say yes."

Jessica nodded. "But I didn't say yes."

"Until he gave you a dragon."

"It wasn't just the dragon, it's what it represents."

"Your lost childhood?" Amy inquired with a teasing grin.

Jessica shook her head, her glowing smile filled with gentle hope. "My lost dreams."

"So how's the battle going?" Joe asked. "Did you win the war yet?"

"Not yet, but I'm getting close to my objective," Curt replied, jiggling the phone against his ear as he signed off on a training report. The metal desk he was sitting at seemed small and confining. He was forever banging his knee on an open drawer or the desk corner. He was a man of action, not a paper-pusher. This was the longest he'd been at a desk since he was in school.

Early on, one of his commanding officers had suggested he consider going in for officer training, but Curt hadn't wanted to leave the adrenaline rush of active duty. Like he'd told Jessica, he'd wanted to see the world. He'd also wanted to keep moving. And when he was in the middle of some hot spot, responsible for the well-being of the men in his platoon, there was no time to brood about his past, no time to listen to those dark voices in his head that whispered he wasn't good enough and never would be.

He'd proved those voices wrong. He knew he was a damn good Marine. The numerous commendations he'd received told him that the U.S. Marine Corps knew it, too.

Now the question was could he be a damn good father…and husband? The jury was still out on that one.

"I've still got a few logistical details to work out yet," Curt told Joe.

"Like what?" Joe asked.

"Like where to take her tonight," Curt admitted.

"Tonight? You're not giving me much lead time, Blackwell."

"You're a fast thinker, Wilder," Curt retorted. "So start thinking."

"What are you looking for here, someplace intimately candlelit with French food?"

"The only French food I like is French fries."

"Scratch that then."

"I was thinking of taking her to that fancy restaurant on top of the John Hancock Building. You ever been up there?''

''Yeah. Good steak and a great view.''

''So you think I should take her there?''

''Jeez, Blackwell, since when do you check with me about where to take your dates? This woman has really gotten to you. I never thought I'd see the day.''

''Sure go ahead and laugh. Just wait until some woman gets under your skin.''

''Lots of women have gotten under my skin,'' Joe retorted. ''That's why I couldn't ever settle down with just one. Besides, you know how high the divorce rate is among Marines. Women don't take kindly to us being Marines first and husbands second.''

''I know, but Jessica is different.''

''She'd have to be to get your attention. So tell me, how's the daddy gig going?''

''Never tell a three-year-old to go out there and kick some butt. They take you literally.'' Curt went on to give Joe an abbreviated version of Blue's ballet debut.

Joe's laughter was hearty. ''At least you didn't tell her that Marine kids are tough and can chew nails. My dad always told me and my brothers that.''

Joe came from a large tight-knit military family, his experience so different from Curt's. Sometimes he thought it was a miracle they were friends. But the Marine Corps had brought them together. That and a similarly wacky sense of humor. Despite their differences, Curt sensed a darker side to Joe that he kept well-hidden.

Not that Curt had ever asked him about it. He figured if Joe wanted to talk, he knew where to reach him. The same was true for him. Curt knew he could depend on Joe.

"Don't forget to invite me to the wedding," Joe said.

"I wouldn't have it without you, buddy."

"That's for damn sure. You just remember that it's been my fine advice that's gotten you where you are today."

"Banged up with a busted leg teaching squibs?" Curt retorted, running his bent knuckles over his achy thigh.

"I meant with Jessica. It's been my wisdom and guidance that's led this operation to success."

"That battle isn't won yet," Curt warned him. "She hasn't said yes yet."

"She will, Blackwell. She will."

Knowing Curt's military precision where punctuality was concerned, she eyed the clock on the hallway table with concern. He was five minutes late. What if something had happened?

He wouldn't have asked her out just to stand her up. No way.

That realization told her a lot about her own trust in Curt. He was an honorable man, who stood by his responsibilities. If he said he'd be here, he'd be here.

Sure enough, her intercom buzzed, indicating there was someone in the lobby. It was Curt.

The last time he was here he'd bypassed the security system by meeting up with Mr. Sanders, who lived at the end of the hallway and had been in the Marines during the Korean Conflict. On his way into the building, Mr. Sanders had naturally kept the door open for a fellow Marine. Jessica wasn't sure who let the pizza deliveryman past the security door in the lobby that day, but she suspected it one of the Sanderses' kids.

Such mundane thoughts kept her from panicking about the short skirt on her dress. The dress was very flattering, its classic lines hugging her body. And her legs looked even longer thanks to the killer strappy shoes she wore. It had been so long since she'd worn such high heels that she'd had to practice walking in them without wobbling. She thought she had it down pat now.

Then she opened the door and saw Curt. This was the fourth time she'd ever seen him in his dress blues. The impact was still awesome.

"Sorry I'm late. Blue took forever to get dressed before I could drop her off at the sitter. We couldn't leave until we found her black patent leather shoes. She refused to wear any other pair. Then she had to put matching shoes on Fooba bear. I thought we'd never get out of my place."

Curt saw her eyeing his uniform and hoped she didn't think he was being pretentious by wearing it. The truth was that he didn't own a suit. He'd never had any need for one. And since the restaurant tonight required a jacket and tie, it was his dress blues or nothing.

Then he got over his own nervousness long enough to notice what she was wearing. Notice was a mild way of putting it. He couldn't take his eyes off her. She was wearing some black clingy dress that followed her curves like a lover's hand. And her legs...

He hoped he wasn't drooling. Her legs went on forever. He was speechless.

She'd used that perfumed shower gel he'd gotten her. He recognized the scent—nice with just a touch of naughty. It suited her so well. Especially tonight.

His gaze lifted to her face. Her honey-blond hair was piled on top of her head in a way guaranteed to make a man want to remove the wide silver clip and make the silky strands tumble around her shoulders. She wore more makeup than usual, making her green eyes look even more gorgeous and her mouth... downright luscious. Her shimmery lipstick was a sinful red, the color of cherries.

"Um..." She licked her lips nervously, as if she, too, was uncertain what to say. "I'm ready to go."

"I'm ready, too," he murmured, stepping closer. "Ready for this."

Gently tipping her chin up, he brushed his lips over hers. She tasted as good as she looked. He truly meant the kiss to be a quick greeting. But his good intentions flew out the window when she responded.

Jessica slid her hand along his jaw, relishing in the fool of his warm skin beneath her fingertips. She couldn't believe how perfect the kiss was, how deliciously exhilarating it was to know that he wanted her. He seemed to know exactly how to please her— where to touch, where to linger, when to deepen the pressure of his mouth on hers, when to add a tempting thrust of his tongue.

In his arms she became a different person, someone capable of arousing the passions of a sexy and powerful man like Curt. She was no longer the awkward teenager who had never experienced love. Instead she was a woman confident of her appeal and her own femininity.

Then her stomach growled. Not a dainty sound, and it startled her so much that she stepped back from him in embarrassment.

"Sorry about that. I skipped lunch," she mumbled self-consciously. So much for being a confident woman in killer heels.

"Don't be embarrassed," he murmured. Taking her hand, he raised it to his lips, palm uppermost, to press a kiss against her skin before folding her fingers over as if to hold the memory of his kiss there. "I'm hungry, too," he told her, his hand sliding down her arm to her elbow before he moved away.

The darkly intense look he gave her told her he was hungry for her, not for food.

Flustered, she grabbed her silky black cardigan sweater, clutched it to her and said, "We should go."

"Affirmative." He straightened as if he were a palace guard and she the resident princess.

Jessica knew they talked on the drive to the John Hancock Building but for the life of her she couldn't remember what was said. Once they were inside the high-speed elevator that whisked them up to the 95th floor, she clung to Curt's arm more for the sheer enjoyment of being so close to him than out of any concern regarding the elevator's safety.

It was a clear night, and the view from their window-side table was impressive. Almost as impressive as Curt in his dress blues. She'd caught the other women eyeing him as they'd walked to their table. Tonight he was all hers.

That realization made it hard for her to concentrate

on anything but Curt. Oh, the magical view of the Outer Drive curling north along the lakefront like a ribbon of lights contributed to the perfect setting. So did the tender steaks and mouthwatering roasted potatoes with tender asparagus spears. But it was Curt who captured most of her attention—the way he gazed at her mouth as if he couldn't wait to kiss her again, the way he listened when she spoke, the way his smile changed the stark lines of his face.

Dessert was a decadent chocolate mousse, but not as decadent as that kiss they'd shared earlier in the evening. He was treating her as if she was a woman he really desired, a woman who was special to him.

The perfect evening continued once they were back outside. There was no wind off the lake tonight to cool things down, so the sidewalks were crowded with people making the most of the unusually warm late April evening.

As they crossed Michigan Avenue to where Curt had parked the car, they passed Chicago's historic Water Tower and the line of horse and buggies waiting for the tourist trade.

Laughing self-consciously, she confessed, "When I was a little girl I used to imagine at Halloween that our pumpkin would turn into Cinderella's coach with a team of prancing white horses."

"There's a white horse right here." He nodded toward a horse decked out in equine finery. "Care to accompany me on a buggy ride, ma'am?" he inquired with princely formality.

"I didn't mean you had to...I wasn't fishing for an invitation."

Putting his index finger to her lips, he halted her unsteady flow of words. "Yes or no?"

"Yes."

He smiled as if he liked her saying yes to him, as if he wanted her to say yes more often.

A lake breeze did kick up once they were in the buggy, lowering the temperature by a good ten or fifteen degrees and requiring her to snuggle next to Curt to stay warm. He made her feel so secure and protected. He made her believe that fairy tales could come true—not just for the popular girls who'd been blessed with beauty and poise, but for an ordinary girl like her.

Not that she was a girl any longer. He also made her very much aware of the fact that she was a woman. A woman who was falling in love with him all over again.

Maybe we could have a future together after all. Maybe he loves me after all. Maybe I should say yes.

The contentment of being held in his arms, cuddling together beneath a plaid blanket as the buggy slowly progressed along the side streets, was undeniable. The clip-clop of the horse's hooves against the pavement mimicked the flip-flop of her heart. Her pulse really started racing when Curt began kissing her, his warm lips traveling across her forehead, skimming her eyebrows to brush her temples. When her eyes drifted closed, he dropped soft kisses on her lids.

Surely this was heaven. Never in her wildest dreams had she imagined that she'd be taking a romantic buggy ride with Curt.

The buggy driver had to clear his throat several times to get their attention and let them know that the buggy had stopped rolling. The ride was over. They were back at the beautifully illuminated Water Tower.

Curt gallantly got out first and held out a hand to assist her. Again she was struck by how powerful he looked.

"You know," she teased him, "all the women in that restaurant tonight were eyeing you."

"They were probably wondering what you were doing going out with a banged-up Marine."

"Does your limp bother you?" she quietly asked.

"Does it bother you?" he countered.

She cupped her hand against his cheek. "Only in that it must have hurt you. Not in any other way."

"It's doing better. Much better than the medics expected. I've been doubling up on the physical therapy so I can return..." He stopped abruptly, as if he'd said too much already.

"Return?" Her hand fell to her side like a stone. The premonition hit her with the force of a Midwestern tornado. No, surely he wasn't considering... "You don't mean returning to active duty, do you?"

His tightly controlled features weren't giving anything away, but she could still read something in his eyes, a conflicted consideration of what to say next.

Her voice rose, as did her panic. "Don't lie to me! That's it, isn't it? You're actually preparing to return to active duty."

"It's my job."

"And who do you think is going to take care of Blue while you're off doing your Marine thing?" Curt didn't have to make a verbal response. She could see the answer in his face. It was an answer that hurt her more with each beat of her heart.

Chapter Eleven

"I don't believe this," Jessica whispered. The betrayal went soul deep. Once again she'd let herself believe that Curt really wanted her for herself only to discover that he was using her. "You thought I'd eventually accept your marriage proposal and take care of Blue for you."

Deny it! The plea was like a scream deep inside her. *Please, please deny it and tell me you love me, that you'd marry me even if you didn't have a daughter.*

He couldn't. The truth was too obvious. She saw that in the way his gaze slid away from hers.

No, he couldn't deny it. Because it was true. All of it. All her worst nightmares.

She'd been used, once again. She was just a means to an end.

Pulling a blanket of detachment around herself, she looked away from Curt to the people walking by—

smiling and laughing as if the world was still a normal place. How appropriate that this final confrontation between herself and Curt should take place in front of the Water Tower, the only thing left standing after the Chicago Fire. A similar conflagration was taking place inside of Jessica. Her dreams of the future were going up in flames right before her very eyes.

Because they'd been dreams based on lies, his lies. Not spoken lies perhaps, but lies nonetheless. Making her believe with his kisses that he wanted her when what he really wanted was a mother for his daughter so he could go off footloose and worry-free while she took care of Blue's needs.

He didn't need Jessica, he needed a nursemaid for his child.

What made you think that this time would be different? That it wouldn't end in heartbreak like before?

You may be older but you're sure not any wiser, are you? Underneath it all, you're still that lonely geeky teenager searching in vain for someone to love her.

She took a step backward as the pain came at her in recurring waves that were nearly overwhelming. The effort of holding herself aloof was taking its toll.

Blinking back the threat of tears, she tried to avoid looking at the man who had stomped on her heart with combat boots. But despite her best intentions, her gaze returned to his face…searching for what she wasn't sure. Regret? Love?

"Don't look at me that way," he bit out.

His words fired her anger. "Don't worry, from now on I don't plan on looking at you at all!"

"Hold on, where are you going?"

He reached for her, she sidestepped him. This was a scene that was becoming all to familiar to her. Him hurting her, her needing to get away. "I'm going to get a cab and go home," she icily informed him. "This con job of yours is over."

"If you want to go home, I'll take you home," he growled.

"No, you won't."

Now his anger bubbled over. "What do you want from me? I gave you your favorite things and it still isn't enough. I'm offering you my daughter, and still it's not enough."

Because he hadn't offered her the one thing she wanted above all else. Love. His love.

"That's right," she replied, her voice vibrating with emotion. "It's not enough! Ever since you got Blue, you've been telling me that you take your responsibilities seriously, but that was all a lie. You just wanted to play Daddy for a few weeks. Now you're getting itchy feet and want more excitement in your life. So you want to go traipsing off again. Never mind what effect it would have on Blue. And don't tell me it's your job, or even your calling. Because it's not the U.S. Marines that's calling you back to active duty, is it? No, it's *you*. It's something inside of you that makes you run when things get too close to the bone. When things get too emotional. Because God forbid the big bad Marine should have a heart, that a warrior should cry."

"A warrior never cries," he said, steel in his voice.

"No, he just makes others cry." Keeping the tears at bay, she walked away and didn't look back.

* * *

"I brought chocolate," Amy declared as she entered Jessica's condo an hour later.

Jessica hugged her best friend before taking the box of Fannie Mae candy. "Thanks for coming right over."

"Are you kidding? What are friends for? You'd do the same for me, and have. You know, I can't help feeling that part of this is my fault. I should have recommended you wear a nun's habit or something instead of that sexy dress."

"It wouldn't have mattered what I wore." Jessica had to pause to angrily swipe away the tears sliding down her cheeks. She'd yanked off that stupid dress the moment she'd gotten home and changed into comfort clothes of heather-gray drawstring pants and a matching T-shirt. "I can't believe I fell for his routine. How stupid am I?"

"You're not stupid," Amy loyally defended her, following Jessica into the living room. "You're in love. Okay, so sometimes that works out to be the same thing, but it's not your fault. You can't help who you fall in love with."

"I don't see why not." On her way to the couch, Jessica grabbed a facial tissue to wipe away the rest of her tears.

"I don't, either, frankly. I just know that life doesn't seem to work out that way all the time."

Curling up on her couch, Jessica focused her attention on opening the box and choosing a candy. "Mmm, dark chocolate with lemon cream center."

"I can't believe Curt had the gall to actually tell

you that he wants you to watch Blue while he returns to active duty.''

"He's smarter than that. I don't think he meant to tell me that he was trying to return to active duty. He let that slip. I was such a fool to believe that he could love me.''

"He's the fool for not loving you.''

"I'm not sure Curt knows how to love,'' Jessica said quietly. "I'm not sure he'll allow himself to love.''

"Then that's his loss.''

"I don't know. If love hurts this much then maybe he's got the right idea after all.'' Reaching into the box, Jessica reached for another candy, a strawberry cream this time. "You know what hurts? That he never really ever saw me for who I am. He just saw me as a solution to a problem he had. He didn't see *me*.'' Jessica pounded a clenched fist against her chest, her voice choked with emotion as the tears started again. "And I grew up with a man who never saw me. My father. Being invisible to someone you love eats away at your soul.'' She scrubbed at her face with another tissue. "I'm not crying just because of Curt. I'm crying because…because those old feelings of not being valued, of not being noticed or loved have come back again. It's stupid I know.''

"Hey, I'll be the judge of what's stupid and what's not,'' Amy declared, her voice warm with empathy.

"I never felt like my father even knew I existed half the time. Then there's Curt.'' She paused, biting her lower lip. "Granted he knows I exist because he knows I'm good with his daughter. And I do love Blue. Who knows, maybe if he'd been honest with me in the beginning and said that he wanted me to take care of Blue while he went back to Bosnia, I might have…''

"What?'' Amy indignantly inserted. "Smacked him upside the head? Because that's what he would have deserved. How could he do this to you and to Blue?''

"Do you know how heartbroken that little girl would be if he went away? What can he be thinking of? Just when I was starting to trust him, just when I was starting to believe that he understood what being a parent really meant, he goes and pulls this.''

"You'll get over him,'' Amy declared.

"When? When I'm ninety? I think he's the devil in my soul, so much a part of me that I can't get rid of him,'' Jessica muttered, reaching for a handful of chocolate creams this time.

"We could perform an exorcism. Or dress up G.I. Joe in frilly dresses. You said that drove him nuts.''

"I did the right thing turning Curt down,'' Jessica said, almost as if wanting to reassure herself.

"You certainly did,'' Amy immediately agreed. "Why? You're not regretting that are you?''

"No. But I can't help thinking about Blue. Here I am considering adopting a child, one I've never met, yet I won't help Blue whom I do truly love.'' Jessica ran her hands through her rumpled hair, before pressing the heels of her hands against her forehead. "This is such a mess.''

"Marrying Curt, loving him the way you do without him reciprocating would tear you up. You said it yourself, it eats away at your soul.''

"Maybe I want too much.''

Amy glared at her. "If you really think you're so undeserving of love then you don't deserve those chocolates. Hand them over!"

Jessica hung onto the box. "No way. Wanting a man who loves me is not wanting too much."

"Darn right."

"You know in preschool the kids are forever playacting. The textbooks call it cooperative pretending. And that's what Curt and I were doing. He was pretending to really care about me and I was pretending it would work out. Playacting."

"At least he showed you his true colors before it was too late."

Curt's true colors were dress blue. It was clear the United States Marine Corps came first with him and always would.

"I want more water," Blue said.

"That's already your third glass."

"Fooba drank those. Read me *The Wishing Tree*." It was her favorite book, about a little girl who grew a magical tree in the woods.

"I already read it to you five times. Now lie down and go to sleep."

She bounced right back up again. "Susan has a kitty, can I have one, too?"

"No."

"Why?"

"Because they don't allow kitties here."

"If my mommy was here, could I have a kitty? How come Susan gets one and not me? 'Cause she has a mommy?"

"No, that's not why."

"Then why?"

"Because I said so."

"I want a kitty."

"So you've already stated. Several times."

"Fooba wants a kitty, too," Blue earnestly assured him.

He was not impressed. "Fooba has no vote in the matter."

"How come?"

"Because Fooba's a teddy bear."

"How come teddy bears can't vote? What's a vote?"

He was not about to go into political matters at this late hour. "It's way past your bedtime. Lights out."

"No! Want more water and a kitty."

"You are a Marine kid and a Marine kid never..." He paused, his look clearly telling her to fill in the rest.

"Never gives up," she dutifully said before adding, "and wants a kitty."

"A Marine kid does not give up and they also do not bellyache. So this aforementioned bad behavior will stop as of right now." The military terminology made him feel better, made him feel more in control of the situation. Unfortunately it didn't make Blue feel any better and showed no signs of working. "Do you read me?"

"No!" She glared at him mutinously. "Want Jessie."

He wanted Jessie, too. From the moment he'd walked into her condo tonight, he'd wanted her. Maybe he'd wanted her from the time he was back in high school, when she seemed too far above him, so unreachable. But tonight, when he'd kissed her, she'd wanted him back.

The courting thing had been working, he was sure of it. He wasn't sure where he'd gone wrong after that.

She'd gone ballistic when he'd talked about rejoining his men in Bosnia. Why couldn't she understand? He was responsible for those forty-five Marines still there.

It wasn't like he wanted to go gambling in Las Vegas or treasure hunting off the coast of Florida or anything. And it wasn't as if he wanted to return to Bosnia because of the great weather or working conditions.

He had something to prove. That he wasn't all washed up. That he wasn't a has-been, a wounded warrior who no longer was able to fulfill his duty.

Warriors never cry, he'd told her.

No they just make others cry. Jessie's words had stayed in his head, refusing to be banished.

He wasn't trying to hurt anyone, he was trying to do what was best here. Blue loved Jessie, she loved Blue—what was the problem? He wasn't trying to palm off his daughter on someone else, he was just looking out for her best welfare. He'd certainly continue to financially support Blue and once his tour was over in Bosnia…

Who was he kidding? Jessie wasn't going to marry him, and odds were that he'd never return to Bosnia. Maybe the medics were right and there was no hope of him returning to active duty. Which would leave him where? Pushing papers for the rest of his enlisted years?

He was a United States Marine. He'd sailed through advanced infantry training. He knew how to survive behind enemy lines for a week without food, how to assess battle techniques and go for an enemy's weaknesses. He knew combat first aid, could carry a fallen comrade over his shoulder to safety, knew how to blend into his surroundings so thoroughly that no one walking within three feet would even see him.

He knew all that. It's what he did. Who he was. Because if he wasn't that, he was nothing.

"Want Jessie!" Blue wailed, the tears starting in earnest this time.

"Jessie's sleeping. The way you should be sleeping."

Blue started crying even harder now.

Warriors never cry, they just make others cry.

She'll stop in a minute, he told himself as he got up and left the room. Remember how she'd cried at the restaurant, or how she had a fit about putting on her shoes earlier tonight. She can turn it off and on at the drop of a hat. It doesn't mean anything. You can't give in to it.

She has to learn. Has to learn that there were rules in life, and one of them was that you didn't always get what you wanted. It was sure a lesson he'd learned himself time and time again. Better that Blue learned now rather than be disappointed later.

"A good teacher recognizes and values different social styles in her students," Jessica reminded herself under her breath first thing Monday morning. "A good teacher does want to string a student up by his shoelaces."

"She does if that student is Brian," Lisa added, looking over Jessica's shoulder as they both gazed down at the bottom desk drawer. It had taken them several minutes to finally locate the source of the awful smell. Thank heavens the kids hadn't arrived yet. "I can't believe he made such a mess. What is it? Rotten eggs?"

"Yes. His eggs were missing from that cooking project we did on Friday. I meant to check more thoroughly...." But she'd been so excited about her date with Curt that she'd forgotten. "You weren't supposed to hear that about hanging him by his shoelaces," Jessica added.

"Hear what?" Lisa said, trailing after her with a handful of egg-soaked paper towels as Jessica got rid of the offending mess in the Dumpster outside. When they returned inside, Tawanna had already taken charge of the rest of the cleanup and opened the windows to air out the room. "What I really want to hear is what you and Curt did Friday night."

"Why should she tell you?" Tawanna glared at Lisa. "You tried to steal her man away from her."

"I was just testing him," Lisa said self-righteously.

"Yeah, right," Tawanna scoffed.

"What about you?" Lisa countered. "I saw you giving him your phone number."

Tawanna shrugged. "The poor man needed my advice. And you know how good I am at giving advice."

"Advice about what?" Jessica demanded.

"Not what, who. Advice about you. Oh, don't worry, I didn't tell him any secrets."

"Well, I did," Lisa said. "I told him about that

thing you have for barbecued potato chips. But only after he grilled me for that information.''

''He grilled you?'' Jessica repeated. ''About me?''

Lisa nodded. ''That's why I was talking to him so clandestinely in the corner.'' Seeing Tawanna's disbelieving look, Lisa admitted, ''Okay, I did very gently try to hit on the guy, but he made it very clear he was only interested in Jessica.''

She laughed bitterly. ''Only interested in me to be a mother to Blue while he goes off into the wild blue yonder.''

''That's actually the Air Force's song,'' Lisa said. Seeing the disapproving look from Tawanna she quickly added, ''Not that it's important.''

''I can't believe that's the only reason he'd be interested in you.'' Tawanna waved her hand in the air for emphasis. With her colorful caftan and her hair wrapped in a matching turban she looked like a vengeful African goddess.

''I didn't want to believe it, either. But he's planning on returning to active duty in Bosnia,'' Jessica said.

''What about Blue?'' Tawanna demanded in outrage.

''What about his limp?'' the ever practical Lisa asked. ''I wouldn't think the Marines would let him return to active duty. Are you sure they're sending him there again?''

''I know he wants to go back,'' Jessica said.

''Well, sure he probably wants to go back.'' Lisa tucked her long black hair behind one ear, her almond-shaped eyes gazing at Jessica in confusion. ''I mean, he's a Marine, that's what he does.''

"He's a father," Jessica said.

"That doesn't mean he can stop being a Marine. It's not exactly a regular nine-to-five kind of job," Tawanna said.

"I really don't think you'll have anything to worry about," Lisa assured her. "I don't think they'll be shipping him back there."

"Meanwhile I just saw him pull up with Blue. Are you gonna be okay?" Tawanna asked.

Jessica nodded. The situation was made easier by the fact that he didn't stay, just dropped Blue off and left without a word to anyone.

It was a very hectic day, which gave her absolutely no time to brood about Curt. She turned her back for a minute and the next thing she knew, the kids had decided to paint with their hands instead of their brushes and had the colorful stuff spread up to their elbows in two seconds flat. She'd barely had time to clean them off before she caught Brian feeding his snack of fish-shaped crackers to the fish in the fish tank, quickly followed by an apple that almost hit a quickly dodging goldfish. In all the chaos, Blue seemed quieter than usual. Jessica tried to get Blue to talk to her, but the little girl just shook her head and clutched her Fooba teddy bear more closely to her chest.

She dreaded having to ask Curt about Blue's behavior but if something had happened over the weekend, other than Curt breaking Jessica's heart, then she should know about it.

When Curt came to pick her up after school, he was in a bad mood. Jessica could tell just by looking at him across the room. Well, bad mood might be the wrong description. He was remote, that might be a better word.

Approaching him, Jessica decided to get right to the point. "How did things go with you and Blue this weekend?"

"Why do you care?" he retorted in a steely voice.

"You know I care about Blue. You used that to your advantage."

"You don't care about Blue. You just care about yourself."

"You're a fine one to be throwing that accusation around," she shot back in an angry undertone.

"Meaning what?" he demanded.

"That you're the one who only cares about yourself."

"It's useless talking to you," he said. "Where's Blue? We're leaving."

"She's..." Turning, Jessica looked at the playacting corner where Blue had been a few moments before. "I don't understand...she was just there a minute ago."

"Are you telling me you've *lost* my daughter?" Curt demanded in an icy voice that sent chills down her spine.

Chapter Twelve

"Of course she's not lost," Jessica said before calling out to Lisa and Tawanna. "Have either of you seen Blue?"

"She was here a minute or two ago," Tawanna replied as Lisa nodded in agreement.

"Well, then she can't have gone far," Jessica said.

But ten minutes of searching showed no results.

Jessica anxiously checked with Blue's friend Susan to see if Blue had said anything to her about going anywhere. Susan's mom was there to pick her up, and had watched Blue on Friday night. "She seemed fine when Curt picked her up," she said.

Turning to Curt, Jessica repeated her earlier question. "Did anything unusual happen over the weekend? Anything that might have upset her?"

Curt's eyes darkened with pain and regret. "She wanted me to call you. She cried when I refused."

"We'll find her," Jessica said.

A staff search party was already in full swing, checking out every corner of the building. Nothing. No sign of Blue.

"What about those woods?" Curt asked. "Where you had that Easter Egg hunt?"

"There's a six-foot high fence around the back play area," Jessica replied. "She couldn't have gotten through that to get into the forest preserve."

Sarah, the preschool director, spoke to Curt and told him what steps were being taken as the search went into full swing.

Meanwhile, Jessica stood in front of the cubbies where the children stored their coats and things. Blue's jacket was gone. The cubbies were marked not only with the child's name but also with a Polaroid photograph. She reached out with trembling fingers to trace Blue's photo.

Jessica remembered the day that photo was taken. It had been Blue's second day in school. Blue had tentatively approached a group of girls in the sandbox and said, "Can I play, too?"

"No," one of the girls had replied. "Go away. We don't want you!"

Before Jessica could intervene, Susan had come to Blue's rescue, putting her arm around her and saying, "Blue is my friend. She can play with me."

It was the beginning of Blue's acceptance.

Where could she be?

Years of military training helped Curt concentrate on what the preschool director was telling him when inside all he wanted to do was scream that this was all his fault. He'd let Blue cry herself to sleep Friday night. And last night, too.

What kind a father lets his kid cry herself to sleep? A rotten one.

What had ever made him think he'd be good enough to be a father?

The preschool director didn't have to tell him how sorry she was about this. He didn't blame her. No, he was the one to blame here. He was the reason Blue was missing. He was the one who'd upset her. He was the one who'd left her to cry alone in the dark. He was the one who stood in this room and was so intent on fighting with Jessica that he hadn't even noticed his own flesh and blood.

She was such a little thing. And he'd let her down. He'd screwed up. Again.

As a kid, he'd been so angry. Bitter, too. At being abandoned by first his father and then his mother, at being dumped like a sack of garbage. That's when he'd vowed that he wouldn't care anymore—about anyone. He wouldn't let anyone get to him. He'd walk away from love if it meant being hurt that badly.

But he couldn't walk away anymore. Not from Blue. Not from his little girl.

What good was all his training if he couldn't track her down? What good was saving the world if he couldn't save his daughter? What good was he without her?

"I'm going to go find her." If she'd gone into those woods, he'd locate her. But he had to get moving. He couldn't just stand around here doing nothing. Time was wasting. Blue needed him. He wouldn't let her down again. "I'm going to go find her."

He felt Jessica's hand on his hand and braced himself for her to tell him that Blue would never have disappeared if he hadn't been so selfish. She wouldn't be telling him anything he didn't already know.

"It's not your fault," she said.

"Yes, it is. I let her cry herself to sleep. She sobbed and I didn't do a thing about it. Not just once, but both Friday and last night. Saturday night she went to sleep just fine and I thought...she'd gotten over wanting to see you. But she hadn't. This is my fault and don't you dare try to tell me it isn't."

His voice sounded frantic, but he didn't care. "She wanted a kitten. That's how it got started. She wanted a kitten because her friend had one. She didn't see why she couldn't have one, too. When I said no, she said she wanted you. Then she started crying. I should have said I'd get her a kitten. As soon as I find her, we'll go get one."

But he didn't find her. Nor did anyone else. Curt checked his watch. She'd been missing for an hour now. It seemed like days. Like years. Desperation was clawing through him. He'd lost her. Lost the one good thing in his life.

He cursed his bum leg for slowing him down, cursed the woods for being so thick, and cursed himself for...everything.

"Where are you, Blue?" Jessica yelled for the hundredth time. "Please answer me!"

She along with at least a dozen other staff members had spread out and were combing the woods. There was a chance that Blue had slipped out a side door to the building that had been mistakenly left unlocked, in which case she could have wandered into the forest preserve. Jessica had tried to keep up with Curt, but he was like a man possessed. Not that she blamed him.

There were so many dangers in this world for small children. What if someone had coaxed her into their car by promising her candy, or saying they had a message from her father? Jessica had covered stranger danger in class, warning the preschoolers not to be lured by those kinds of tactics. But Blue was only three. Would she remember those lessons?

Jessica tried to reassure herself with the knowledge that Blue was naturally very wary of strangers. And today the little one had been especially withdrawn.

Odds were that she'd just wandered off exploring, rather than being lured away. But again, Blue wasn't the kind of child to fearlessly go off into the unknown. She'd already had too much upheaval in her young life to feel that confident about heading off on an adventure.

Jessica continued her search, her voice becoming hoarse from shouting. It would be twilight soon. They had to find Blue before darkness fell. At least she had her jacket with her, the air was turning just a bit cooler now. Thankfully the early May day had been a warm one.

She heard a twig snap a short distance away. Praying it was Blue, she rushed over, only to find Curt. "Did you find her?"

He shook his head, keeping his face turned away from Jessica. Something about his stance warned her that this was a man on the ragged edge. The camouflage uniform he wore blended into the woods around them, but the tension emanating from his body was clear to see.

"Curt?" She put her hand on his shoulder, turning him to face her. His red-rimmed eyes were self-condemning and filled with desperation.

This battle-tested Marine who vowed that warriors never cry was on the verge of tears.

"Oh, Curt." She slid her arms around him without a second's hesitation. "It's not your fault."

He shuddered once before hugging her as if she were the only sane thing in an insane world. The intensity of his despair was a tangible thing. "I'm a rotten father," he whispered raggedly.

"You're not. You've done so well with Blue. I know it hasn't been easy for you. But you didn't walk away from the challenge of taking care of your daughter. You've studied, you've learned, you've worked hard to let her know that you love her."

"How can she know when I've never told her?" he fiercely countered, stepping away from her to angrily wipe away any hint of wetness from his eyes. "The same way I've never told you."

"Told me what?" Jessica asked.

"That I love you," he said, his voice raw.

Her heart stopped. She never expected this. Not from a man who guarded his emotions so zealously. Yet now that the steel curtain had been lowered, she realized that maybe the reason Curt did guard his emotions was that they ran so deep. The discovery was like a missing key that unlocked the mystery that had always been Curt Blackwell.

"But that doesn't matter." His throat muscles convulsed. "I end up *destroying* the people I love."

Another part of the puzzle.

"Look at me." She firmly turned his tortured face to hers. "Listen to me. You had no way of knowing Blue would take off this way. I know you'd walk over hot coals to save someone you love."

Curt felt her words wash over him. He knew the first rule in combat first aid was to start the breathing and stop the bleeding. But there didn't seem any way to stop the bleeding inside of him at the thought of Blue in danger. As for breathing…he couldn't breathe easily until she was found.

"What if she's never found?" He tried to swallow. Even saying the words was like slicing open an artery. "Kids disappear every day in this country."

"A Marine never gives up," Jessica reminded him.

"She wouldn't settle down," he said, trying to shove away his fear. Giving in to his emotions wasn't going to get Blue back safely. "Kept asking for another glass of water. Wanted me to read her another story."

"Any story in particular?"

"*The Wishing Tree* is her favorite. It's about a little girl who grew a magical tree… Wait a minute! What if she went into the woods looking for the wishing tree? In the book it's the tallest tree around." His gaze instantly searched the top of the woods, until he found one tree that stood larger than the rest.

"Go on," Jessica told him. "I'll be right after you."

Curt reached the tree, a huge oak, just as twilight fell. And there she was, curled up underneath it.

"Blue!" His voice was so thick it was unintelligible. "Blue, are you okay?"

His daughter sat up, gave him a sleepy smile and rubbed her eyes with one hand while clutching her grungy teddy bear with the other. "You found my wishing tree."

She was okay. He ran his hands over her arms and legs to reassure himself. She was okay. Looking past her, his blood chilled when he saw the nearby stream. Shaken, he realized how easily she might have slipped on its banks and fallen in.

Jessica ran into the small clearing in time to see that Curt had literally been brought to his knees as he knelt and fiercely hugged Blue while telling her over and over that he loved her.

"I love you, too, Daddy," she said with a shy grin. "And I love Jessie."

"I love her, too," Curt said, turning his head to gaze at Jessica with his heart in his eyes. "And I'm not leaving the two of you ever again. If that means leaving the Marines, so be it." Shakenly smiling at Jessica, he said, "While I'm still on my knees, I'm asking you to marry me. Again. Not because of Blue, but because I love you."

"I—" she began when he interrupted her.

"Look, I know I'm no prize," he quickly said, as if he couldn't get the words out fast enough. "The other day you accused me of having something inside of me that makes me run when things get too emotional. You were right. You know my family history. After my parents dumped me I vowed that I wouldn't care anymore—about anyone. I refused to let anyone get to me and swore I'd walk away rather than get hurt that way again. But I can't walk away anymore. Not from Blue. And not from you, Jessie."

She'd always been able to read the truth in his eyes, when he let his guard down enough to allow her to see through to his heart. He did so now. Curt had learned the hard way what love was all about, and it had brought her proud warrior to his knees before her.

Her own shaky legs gave out as she sank onto the ground beside him. "I don't want you to walk away. I never did. I love you, Curt. And I'd be honored to marry you."

As he kissed her, she vaguely heard Blue clapping her hands and saying, "My wishing tree made my wish come true!"

"It made my wish come true, too," Jessica whispered against Curt's lips.

Epilogue

Three months later...

"Why didn't you tell me Curt's best friend looks like Mel Gibson?" Amy demanded. "Are you sure you're marrying the right Marine today?"

"Positive," Jessica replied as she looked in the full-length mirror and adjusted the bodice of her white wedding dress. With its dainty lace along the sweetheart neckline and bell-like skirt, it was a gown for a princess. Staring at herself, she still had a hard time believing that was her. "And I hadn't met Joe myself until the rehearsal dinner last night."

"I can't believe how calm you are. In just a few minutes you'll be walking down the aisle and becoming Curt's wife."

"And he'll become my husband." She said the words with such a sense of satisfaction that Amy smiled.

"It's great seeing you so happy."

"Blue has her wishing tree, and I've got my dragon." Jessica patted the head of the dragon Curt had given her. She'd brought it to the church with her, to remind her how lucky she was. "You were right. I should have gone in for a complete checkup from a specialist earlier rather than taking my family doctor's word for my condition. Especially since he wasn't up on the latest information. But I never wanted to deal with it…anyway I still am so excited with the news. A tipped uterus is a small risk factor but nothing insurmountable. I can have children after all." Jessica did a little dance around a footstool.

"So name the first one after me," Amy said. "Only if she's a girl of course."

"You've got it."

"Did I thank you for asking me to be your maid of honor?" Amy said.

"As if I'd ask anyone else."

"I think Tawanna would have liked the job," Amy noted with a grin.

"Tawanna would never wear a pastel color for a bridesmaid's dress. No, she's much happier being in the audience. She told me she'd be easy to spot, that she'd be sitting right on the aisle. And I hear Lisa is bringing that new boyfriend of hers. He's some kind of Web site creator with a very promising future."

"I think this should be a very interesting wedding. On the bride's side, an array of preschoolers along with their parents. And on the groom's side, a platoon of United States Marines, all in their dress blues. I think I'm going to cry when you walk under that canopy of sabers. A full-dress Marine wedding. I think even your mom will be impressed.''

"I'm just glad she got back from her cruise in time."

"Speaking of time..." Amy tapped her delicate gold watch meaningfully. "Are you ready?"

Jessica grinned. "Affirmative."

The minute Jessica began her walk down the aisle, she didn't notice anything but Curt, waiting for her near the altar. Hearing laughter, she saw that Blue, who was adorably dressed as a flower girl, had paused to lean down and pick up Fooba bear who was wearing a bridal veil. The little girl then continued on her way, tossing flower petals with a throw that would no doubt make Curt proud, and think she should try out for the major leagues.

Then her attention returned to Curt, who looked even more dashing than usual in full-dress blues. She felt the warmth of his fingers through the white gloves he wore, felt the conviction of his gaze as he looked at her and let her see how much he loved her.

The ceremony was a blur to her, but she'd never forget that look in his eyes. Or what happened once the minister declared them husband and wife. The church erupted with a series of *ooohrahs!* from the Marines quickly followed by the mayhem of squealing preschoolers.

And as Jessica and Curt kissed as husband and wife for the first time, the sound of "You Can't Hurry Love" sung by ex-Genesis member Phil Collins filled the church.

* * * * *

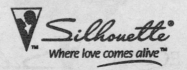

**Don't miss
an exciting opportunity
to save on the purchase of
Harlequin and Silhouette books!**

Buy any two Harlequin or
Silhouette books and save
$10.00 off future Harlequin
and Silhouette purchases

OR

buy any three
Harlequin or Silhouette books
and save **$20.00 off** future
Harlequin and Silhouette purchases.

**Watch for details
coming in October 2000!**

PHQ400

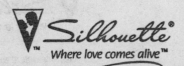

COMING NEXT MONTH